What the critics are saying...

"Ms. Wine had me sitting on the edge of my seat. Just when I thought everything was going to be okay, another twist, then a turn would come by. I did not want to put it down. Simple, go out and read this book." ~ *Darnce Coffee Time Romance*

"Beyond Boundaries is a book for all readers looking for a great story!" ~ *Dani Jacquel Just Erotic Romance Reviews*

MARY WINE

BEYOND BOUNDARIES

ELLORA'S CAVE
ROMANTICA PUBLISHING

An Ellora's Cave Romantica Publication

www.ellorascave.com

Breaking Boundaries: Beyond Boundaries

ISBN #1419952226
ALL RIGHTS RESERVED.
Beyond Boundaries Copyright© 2005 Mary Wine
Edited by: Sue-Ellen Gower
Cover art by: Syneca

Electronic book Publication: January, 2005
Trade paperback Publication: July, 2005

Excerpt from *Dream Specter* Copyright © Mary Wine, 2004
Excerpt from *Dream Surrender* Copyright © Mary Wine, 2005

Warning:

The following material contains graphic sexual content meant for mature readers. *Beyond Boundaries* has been rated *S-ensuous* by a minimum of three independent reviewers.

Ellora's Cave Publishing offers three levels of Romantica™ reading entertainment: S (S-ensuous), E (E-rotic), and X (X-treme).

S-ensuous love scenes are explicit and leave nothing to the imagination.

E-rotic love scenes are explicit, leave nothing to the imagination, and are high in volume per the overall word count. In addition, some E-rated titles might contain fantasy material that some readers find objectionable, such as bondage, submission, same sex encounters, forced seductions, etc. E-rated titles are the most graphic titles we carry; it is common, for instance, for an author to use words such as "fucking", "cock", "pussy", etc., within their work of literature.

X-treme titles differ from E-rated titles only in plot premise and storyline execution. Unlike E-rated titles, stories designated with the letter X tend to contain controversial subject matter not for the faint of heart.

Also by Mary Wine:

Beyond Boundaries
Breaking Boundaries

Chapter One

"Now even you must admit that that one would make a strong mate."

Nacoma made the statement but all four heads turned toward Chenoa. Lifting her eyes she let them wander over the man in question.

To say the man was strong was an understatement. He was sculpted to perfection. The men were wrestling in the rising morning heat. With a circle drawn in the dirt they would try to force their opponent over the boundary to claim victory. Their powerful legs strained as they dug their feet into the dirt and used their strength to hold each other at bay.

"Ah, you see, Chenoa does think he is handsome."

The women laughed and Chenoa turned her head toward her friend. "Nacoma, why do you ask questions that don't need to be answered?"

The women laughed again and so did Chenoa. There was nothing wrong with Nacoma's mischief. Raising her eyes toward the men again, Chenoa considered them. They were all strong. Each one was an image of male perfection.

These men had competed across the globe for the chance to be on the reservation. The arenas these men came from molded them into warriors. The competition was fierce. But the current match was for display only. They were bragging with their bodies as they tried to entice the young women of the tribe into their beds.

But Chenoa only knew that from stories. She'd been born on the reservation and had never been allowed to set foot off it. Mother Earth had begun taking her revenge against the human race that had raped her. Pollution across the globe had produced a rather ironic justice.

Less then two percent of all females born were fertile. Modern science was baffled. But here life didn't adopt that same fate. The reservation was still unpaved and the houses still simple.

Most importantly, there were still children here. Reaching out, Chenoa rubbed the swollen mound of Nacoma's belly. The unborn baby kicked and Chenoa smiled.

"You see, even this child thinks you should go and meet that one. Your baby could become playmates with mine." Nacoma nodded her head and smiled. Chenoa lifted her eyes to the arena again. She would adore a child. Her grandmother would simply burst with pride.

But there was something so cheap about picking out a father for her child like this. She knew why it was allowed but she was also certain her ancestors were going to haunt her if she ever even thought about taking one to her bed.

Chenoa stood up and left the group. Suddenly the entire thing became very ugly. She wandered down the road and nodded to those who passed her. The reservation was simple. Most people in the outside world called it primitive.

Maybe it was primitive but it was also clean. Garbage didn't litter the roadside and the water was still sweet. The air was warm today and Chenoa picked her feet up faster. Noontime would bring a blazing sun that she didn't want to be walking in.

The reservation covered only two hundred square miles. It was a combination of most of the surviving American Indian tribes. They'd been mixed together as urban developers had demanded the Indian land. It was really strange how they were being punished for their greed now.

Chenoa considered the road in front of her that led to the modern world. The boundary between the Indian world and the outside world was marked by a twenty-foot-high electric fence that glowed blue in the morning sunlight but, at night, lit up the sky. Her grandmother detested the thing. Chenoa wasn't sure how she felt about it.

The fact was, the fence protected her. On the other side, enforcers patrolled the length of fence to keep potential raiders out. That had become necessary as modern science failed to unravel the mystery of the epidemic of female sterility.

It had been the maternity clothing stores that noticed it first. Their sales had simply stopped. But no one listened 'til the maternity wards became vacant. Next it had been the daycare centers and then the preschools.

Thirty years later, the outside world had an aging population where a fertile woman was worth more than her weight in platinum. There had been other societies that didn't suffer the same fate as the modern, white man's' world. The peace-loving Amish women still bore children.

They had been the first targets of the raiders.

Everyone simply called them raiders. Chenoa called them demons. A new breed of burden, these men didn't simply confine their evil to the Indians. The Amish had been their first targets because they refused to use violence to defend themselves.

It took less than three years to wipe the Amish people from the face of the planet. Quakers, Peacemakers and all of the societies that time seemed to have forgotten were slaughtered for their women.

The government had acted quickly after that. Her people had lived behind the fence ever since. Her grandmother called it a prison, another way the modern man had stolen from the tribe. Chenoa didn't know what to call it. The fence had been there the day she was born. It was simply part of her life.

It would always be a part of her life.

If she labeled it a prison then she was a captive. That just seemed a rather poor choice to make. After all, if one was a captive then shouldn't one yearn for freedom?

Freedom was the last thing on Chenoa's mind—all she wanted right now was a cool drink. Her house came into view and she quickened her pace again. She stomped her feet on the porch to knock the dirt off them before she stepped into the front room.

"Chenoa, is that you?"

"Yes, Nacoma sends her greetings and her child is kicking strongly this morning." Chenoa pulled her shoes off and left them by the door. She smiled as her bare feet crossed the wood planking on the floor. Now she was much cooler. Bare feet felt so much better on a hot morning.

The screen door on the back porch squeaked as her grandmother came into the kitchen to see her. Chenoa reached for a cup to fill with the water she'd been thinking about for the last half hour.

"Nacoma's child is a blessing." Her grandmother considered her from half-closed eyes. "But it is shameful to take a man's seed from his family. Even from a man who believes winning games is a task to devote his life to."

The older woman turned and returned to her garden. Chenoa watched as she tended the plants with years of experience. Her grandmother disapproved of the men and their reason for being on the Peoples' land.

Nacoma had chosen the father of her child in the ring but the child belonged to the tribe and to Nacoma. It was an imperfect solution to the problem the reservation shared with the modern men.

The raiders had come to the reservation. But the Indians weren't as docile as the Amish. Every woman who had been stolen came at a high price.

So they had killed anyone who tried to stop them and now there were few husbands to be found among the members of the tribe. But allowing the men onto the tribal land would ensure the next generation. In twenty years there would be plenty of couples on the reservation but that was going to be too late for her. If Chenoa wanted a child she would have to make the choice to go to the ring for the father.

Chenoa's grandmother didn't like the idea of her taking one of the competitors to her bed but the alternative was to go childless. Reality wasn't kind. Instead it presented her with imperfect solutions. Chenoa watched her grandmother and silently prayed for deliverance.

Reaching for her hat, Chenoa went to help her grandmother. She didn't need to worry so much about it. She was only twenty-two. There was time to let the matter rest. It wasn't just her decision that mattered anyway. If she went to one of the competitors for a child, her grandmother would help her raise it. There were no other living members of her family now.

Chenoa wasn't ignorant. She knew it was only because the scientists still didn't know why the sterility plague still existed. There were endless studies and money was given to the doctors so that even more studies could be undertaken.

The only thing that was certain was the reservation was where babies were being born. So, the babies stayed behind the fence so that the human race wouldn't become extinct.

Reaching for a tomato vine, Chenoa caught its strong spicy scent. She carefully wove it through the fence so that it could support the fruit that it would bear in another month. There was peace in the chore. She'd done this every season since she could walk and she would do it the next season.

Guidance would come and tell her when it was time for another set of hands to join the family labor. Her grandmother began softly chanting and Chenoa joined her. It was a prayer chant. Her grandmother was asking for wisdom from the heavens.

"Someday, my granddaughter, I hope you will understand the joy of love." The old woman took up her prayer chant again and Chenoa waited for her to finish. She lifted her weathered face and smiled at her across the tomato vines. "A child should be born of love."

Chenoa considered her grandmother's words but found herself confused. "Nacoma loves her child so much it shines though her eyes more each morning."

"Yes. Yes." Her grandmother nodded and raised a single finger to point at her. "But there is no love in her heart for a husband. She would be twice as blessed if her child was not born simply from lust. It takes both joys to unite the soul."

The old woman dropped her eyes to her work and began chanting again. Chenoa felt her heart grow heavy. Her grandmother was very wise. There were no husbands to be had, only the competitors.

If her grandmother was right, there could never be any unity for her soul.

* * * * *

Chenoa went to market early the next morning. She didn't want to see the competitors, not today. Her dreams had been filled with images and she couldn't understand them. Instead she found her nerves unsteady as she walked into the market square.

Her eyes focused on the ring and lingered there. It was empty now because it was barely past sunrise. Chenoa stepped forward and looked closer at the ring. There wasn't much to see, just the hard dirt, but she let her eyes consider the spot anyway.

Had Nacoma struggled with her decision so greatly? That was a very good question. Nacoma was two years older than Chenoa was. Maybe her friend had also had such troubling thoughts.

The market was the center of the reservation. Fresh food would be sold here and everyone came into the square in the early morning. Already there were people arriving. But it was still early.

A sharp whistle caught her attention. Chenoa raised her head. In front of her was one of the long buildings that the competitors lived in while on the Peoples' land. They came for a month at a time. The tall man Nacoma had been pointing out yesterday was standing in front of the building watching her.

A smile appeared on his face as she looked at him. But it wasn't a friendly smile. He raked his eyes down her body. It was a slow inspection that lingered on her breasts. As he finished, he jerked his head in invitation before he ran his tongue over his lips.

Chenoa felt her face explode with color. She pressed her lips together and shook her head in refusal. The man laughed and blew her a kiss before he ran his hand over the crotch of his pants. He rubbed the bulge of his sex and jerked his head at her again.

Chenoa turned her back on him. His laughter followed her as she turned toward home. She wouldn't stay anywhere near that creature! Just the way he used his eyes made her feel dirty. She could never bare her breasts for someone like that. His eyes looked on her with less respect than a dog held for a bitch.

"Chenoa? Where are you going?" Nacoma's sunny voice came from the large fountain that was off to the east side of the square. Once it had been the town well but, now that water was pumped to all the residents on the reservation, it had been transformed into a large fountain.

Nacoma stood with her nieces and nephews. There were six children all intent on soaking each other in the morning sunlight. Her friend smiled brightly before walking toward her. Her smile faded as she looked into Chenoa's face.

"What is it?" That same sharp whistle came from behind her and Chenoa felt her temper rise in response. Nacoma raised her face to look at the man. She muttered under her breath before hooking her arm through Chenoa's and pulling her toward the fountain where they would be blocked from the man's view.

"Ignore him. He is just a competitor."

Nacoma rubbed her belly and offered a sad smile toward Chenoa. For the first time, Chenoa noticed the lack of sparkle in her friend's eyes. She simply didn't understand it. Just letting that man look at her body seemed filthy. Her skin was itching for a hot shower to clean it away.

"How did you let one of them touch you?"

Nacoma lifted her hand and pointed toward the children. They were using their shoes to fling water at each other. Delighted squeals filled the morning. "It was not a question of how, but of why. You can do anything if the reason is good enough." Nacoma raised her large dark eyes and Chenoa saw them sparkle with tears instead of joy. Nacoma looked back at the children and raised her head with resolution. "I will never think of it again."

Hopelessness followed Chenoa home. Her grandmother's words floated across her memory and so did the look in Nacoma's eyes. But what she thought about the most was the children that had played all morning in the water.

The house seemed too quiet. Everything was too neat and orderly. A child brought life to a family. But she still felt how dirty that competitor's eyes felt on her breasts. The idea of letting him touch her was revolting.

Her heart was still heavy as she got into bed that night. Heavy with longing, heavy with frustration. There didn't seem to be any way for Chenoa to seek out satisfaction. But the biggest problem was, she still didn't know exactly what it was that she was longing for.

Too many questions clouded her mind. Sleep was nothing but a distant mirage. Chenoa tossed the blanket aside and rose from her bed before the moon was even halfway across the sky.

She kept her feet light as she crossed the floor. Her grandmother needed her sleep. Besides, Chenoa didn't want to explain herself. How could she anyway? She didn't understand why she was so worried about it suddenly.

It must be the approach of Nacoma's baby's birth. Chenoa nodded her head and reached for a glass from the cabinet. Nacoma was like a sister to her and, as her time approached, she was nervous. That had to be the reason. Once the baby was born, all would be well.

Yes. That was it. Chenoa felt the tension leave her thoughts and a smile lift her lips. The baby would be born and everything would be well. Nacoma was the oldest in her group of friends. It was their first true taste of such a difficult decision. All things were troubling the first time you had to face them. Time would bring the greatest solution.

Setting the glass back onto the shelf, she turned back toward her bed.

"Hello, Pretty."

Chapter Two

"She's feisty!" The pig who held her said it like a compliment. Chenoa strained against his hold and tried to kick him. He shoved her against the kitchen counter and pressed his body against hers as he shoved a wad of fabric into her mouth.

"Well, don't take all day about it! Tie her up already. I don't need no brother coming in here to deal with."

Chenoa tried to spit out whatever he'd put into her mouth. Instead he wrapped something else around her head and tied it tight. Her hair got tangled up in the knot and he pulled it ruthlessly.

"Here, I've got her feet." With one huge man pressing her to the counter, her legs were pinned and useless. A hard grip yanked them forward as she heard the small click of metal. Her ankles were held together by something she couldn't budge.

Her hands would be next and Chenoa frantically flailed them at her captor. The man laughed again and she curled her fingers into talons.

"Damn!"

"Shut up!"

"She scratched me." But the man dropped his voice and wrenched her arms around her back. That same click came again and Chenoa felt panic grip her. She refused to accept capture and she withered against her bonds.

"Let's get her out of here."

The man flung her over his shoulder carelessly. Her stomach exploded with pain as she was dropped over the hard bone of his shoulder. "Yah, it's payday."

"Be careful with her, would ya?"

"Shut your yap, she's tougher than both of us together. They live like animals here. Survival of the strongest. You need to make sure she understands who the master is here. She'll give us hell all the way into town otherwise. Just like training a bitch, a few well-aimed kicks and she'll fall right into line."

His words unleashed her panic completely. Despite the pain, Chenoa pulled her body up off of his shoulder. She heard him curse before he lowered her to her feet. Chenoa lunged away from him but he caught her forearm and held her in place. Even in the dark she saw his arm lift and the fist come sailing right into her face.

It didn't hurt because blackness exploded across her vision in the same instant that he hit her.

* * * * *

"Sir?"

A black-gloved hand was held up in response. Both men fell silent as they waited for their commander to direct them. Lee Tanner considered the ground before he looked back at his small computer terminal.

The fluctuation in the fence read as clear as day but that wouldn't be enough information for him to find his deviants tonight. Someone had crossed the fence with the aid of a transfuser. The newest pirate technology warped the magnetic field of the perimeter fence.

But unless he could find the actual unit, he wouldn't know exactly where they had crossed onto the reservation.

And it was one long fence.

His eyes searched the ground looking for the marks left from booted feet. Maybe these pirates had the latest technology but that didn't mean a little good old-fashioned tracking couldn't catch them.

Lee saw the marks. The sod was compressed and broken to show the darker, moist soil beneath. He followed the tracks as they moved along the fence border. The last track was pointing into the fence.

"This is their crossing point." His men began searching for the transfuser unit. It would be a key piece of evidence to convict their suspects. Enforcing the laws on the reservation perimeter was difficult. The pirates who came after the Indians were ruthless and often vaporized their victims to ensure no evidence at a trial.

Crossing the fence was a crime but not an execution crime. Capturing an Indian woman was a transgression that carried the penalty of death. Otherwise there wouldn't be a single female under the age of forty left on the reservation. They were simply worth too much money.

Death was the only penalty high enough to keep the gangs of raiders at a controllable number.

"Dig in. Let's get the job done right tonight."

"Yes, sir."

His men began concealing themselves. Lee considered the surrounding foliage with a critical eye. He was only going to get one chance tonight. There wasn't a single doubt in his mind that these deviants would vaporize their captive the second his men tried to arrest them.

There wasn't much cover to be had. These were experienced pirates. They'd chosen a spot where it would be easy to detect any presence from the enforcers. So that left only the fence. Considering the tracks again, he stood a bare inch from the fence. With his back to the magnetic barrier, Lee felt his hair stand on end. But the deviants would most likely be looking forward.

That was a gamble. If he got knocked into the fence, he'd be dead in about fifteen seconds. But Lee wasn't willing to risk the fact that they might toss their captive into the fence when his men came up out of the desert floor.

Lee kept his eyes on his small palm-sized terminal. The only warning he'd get would be the fluctuation of magnetic waves as the pirates crossed back through the barrier. By the time he saw it, they'd be in front of him. His muscles tightened as he waited to spring his trap.

Wading through that magnetic current brought Chenoa completely awake. Every nerve in her body erupted into sensation that was searing in its intensity. Her eyes sprang open and screamed in protest. The intense blue that lit up the sky even during the daylight caused her pupils to contract in agony.

Two seconds later they'd crossed to the outside world. The sting of her nerves became a dull throbbing. Chenoa opened her eyes but saw nothing but flashes of blue. Suddenly her body became airborne. Bound as she was, Chenoa simply fell to the earth in a boneless heap. Pain hit her as her chin bounced on the hard ground. Sand immediately filled her eyes and she shut them tightly to protect them.

Someone kicked her. A solid boot hooked her midsection and brutally sent her flying across the desert floor. Chenoa was helpless as her body tumbled.

"Welcome to my border." Lee smashed his fist into his suspect's face. The man pitched away from him and he followed. Another solid kick and he fell to his knees. Lee wrenched the man's arms behind him and snapped his own pair of hand restraints onto him.

A look over his shoulder told him their captive was lying some ten feet away. Her chest rose and fell with great heaves as she struggled to escape. Tears were streaming down her cheeks from pain but it was the sweetest sight he'd seen in a long time.

Using his booted foot, Lee kicked his man to the ground. Another swift motion and the man was secured at the ankles as well. There would be no vaporizations on his watch. A side glance told him Xan was cheerfully securing a second suspect for them.

"Xan, we need a transport."

"Ten-four, sir."

Chenoa reacted in terror to the next touch. She knew pain would quickly follow and she twisted in a vain effort to escape. Pain came just with the movement. Her entire body hurt so much. Chenoa felt more tears squeeze out of her eyes and she simply couldn't stop them.

Her eyes sprang open but she still couldn't see. But she could hear him. The man ran a gloved hand over her face and into the hair. The strands screamed as they were pulled. A moan escaped the gag and her tormentor stopped.

"I'm an enforcer. Relax."

Chenoa tried to understand him but her senses were all disjointed and off balance. She could feel the solid hold of the man who held her but her ears told her she was spinning around like a child's toy. Her ears rang and her eyes showed her nothing but flashes of blue.

Her hair was pulled again but she didn't moan. Too many things hurt and there just didn't seem to be any way to express the agony. Her muscles began to spasm and she jerked away from the added pain.

Lee finally pulled the gag out of her mouth. He muffled a curse as her body twitched and convulsed. The magnetic field generated by the fence wasn't designed for human flesh to cross through it. Both pirates had on rubber suits that shielded them from the course of electromagnetic particles.

But they didn't give a damn if their captive had to endure the agony. His requested transport arrived and lit the scene. The light washed over his victim and this time he let the curse slip out.

She was one hell of a mess. The crunch of gravel announced the approach of his lieutenant. Xan stooped down and considered their rescued captive.

"Congratulations, Lee. She's the first surviving one we've had in five years."

"Yeah, well I doubt she's feeling real grateful about it right now."

Someone picked her up and Chenoa felt her last grip on reality leave her. Feeling the solid desert floor beneath her had given her the power to ignore the spinning signals her ears were giving her. Now it was gone and she felt like her body was strapped to a kite as the wind blew it about like an autumn leaf.

Nausea quickly seized her and she doubled over with the new agony. At least her feet were dropped back to earth as she bent over and emptied her stomach. She was bent right over a solid arm but didn't have the strength to refuse the support. She couldn't control the nausea. She couldn't control anything.

She was pulled off the ground again and the world spun her around. Time seemed endless 'til Chenoa finally let herself slip into oblivion.

* * * * *

"You don't have enough to convict us on, Enforcer."

Lee ignored his suspects. Held inside the office's meager restraining cellblock, both men prowled the confines of their cell and tried to keep their panic at bay.

Lee was looking forward to their panic. Standing up, he smiled as both suspects jumped toward the back of their cell. He shook his arms out and flexed his fingers till the knuckles cracked. Both men visibly paled.

"You can't lay a finger on me." His suspect's bravado fell short as the man's eyes frantically searched for escape.

Lee curled his fingers into a fist and grinned. The man shut his mouth like a raw recruit. Only this was scum and Lee was going to build a case so tight even someone like this sludge couldn't ooze out of the cracks.

Right now, Lee needed evidence. Every little piece would help. The enforcer station was equipped with top-notch image and sound recording. It was time to see if he could shake a little self-incriminating information out of his suspect.

Lee used his fist to hit the panel that controlled the restraining field. The amber wall of light went dead and the dull buzz that accompanied it stopped. His suspects tried to climb up the solid concrete wall that made up the back portion of the cell.

"You want to talk? Let's hear it." Lee leaned into the wall and crossed his arms over his chest. One man shook his head violently and plastered himself flat against the wall. The second looked at the open cell door and back to Lee with frantic movements that betrayed his guilt.

This pirate knew what was coming and was desperate to save his own neck. Lee set his teeth together and watched the man. Panic wasn't something to take lightly. His suspect stepped forward and faced off with him.

"You got nothing on me. I wasn't holding that bitch." His nostrils flared and he tossed his head as he shifted his weight from side to side. His forehead was beaded with sweat. Lee looked for all the tiny signs that a body gave off when it was stressed. The man's skin was ruby red as he tried to talk his way out of a felony conviction. The simple fact that he had been helping to abduct the female was grounds for conviction. But Lee would be happy to listen to the man talk. Maybe he'd spill some good information, if he thought it might save his neck.

Lee felt his eyes harden to pinpoints. The suspect's neck was marked with long scratches that were scabbed over now. But they were fresh. He punched the cell restraint and watched it restore the containment field.

"Wait! You have to let me go!" His companion immediately voiced his displeasure at being left to fend for himself. Their voices rose in angry tones and Lee continued on his way down the hall. Maybe they'd kill each other and save him the trouble of delivering them for trial.

He could hope anyway.

Lee slowed his approach as he neared the command office area. Right now, their victim was using it as a makeshift bedroom. All they had at the station was a cot and a couple of jackets but it would have to do. She wasn't in any condition to be moved, much less questioned.

But as far as he knew it wasn't any worse than the living conditions on the reservation. The Indians were a primitive society. In fact, there were a few experts who considered them unable to learn at the same rate as modern humans. Learning was accelerated with the use of growth hormones in the modern world but the native tribes that lived on the reservation refused to use that technology.

"Looking for me?" Xan was in the tiny kitchen that served the station. The man was his second-in-command as well as the medical officer for the station. The reservation was in a remote area and the closest medical facility was over two hundred miles away.

Not that they could take their guest there anyway. The Indians had very harsh opinions about modern man's medicine. Her own people might not accept her back if she was taken to the medical center for treatment.

The situation was a lot like finding a chick that had fallen out of its nest. It was necessary to tend to its injuries or the animal might not survive in its natural environment. On the other hand, if you handled it, its own mother might reject it, possibly even kill it.

"She scratched one of them. Deep."

"Excellent." Xan lowered his coffee mug and went back into the office where his patient was. Lee followed and watched him gently lift both of the girl's hands. His eyes inspected her fingernails. He let a whistle out and held her right hand up for a better look.

"Hand me that bag, sir. Looks like she got him good."

Lee took her wrist instead and Xan nodded. Collecting the samples from beneath her fingernails had to be done by an expert or, in this case, the closet thing they had.

Her wrist was firm but small. His hand closed over it completely. Xan pulled his evidence kit from his pack and began preparing an evidence slide. They'd match the DNA and, with the girl's testimony, these pirates wouldn't be back.

"What are you doing to me?" Chenoa spoke softly as pain sliced into her head like needles. Her body would cramp any time she tried to move so she simply lay as still as possible. Someone held her wrist in a solid grip but she forced herself to relax. Moving that arm would cause the muscles to stiffen and cramp. She just couldn't take any more pain.

But she was balanced on the edge of panic. The horrible fear that she wasn't on the reservation filled her head. No one ever came back from outside the blue fence.

"Any idea what she said?"

"None, sir."

Their language pushed her over that edge and into despair. There wasn't any doubt where she was any more. Chenoa felt the slide of tears from her eyes and tried to decide what to do. There must be a way to get home.

"I speak your language. Please tell me what you are doing."

Her English was heavily accented. It almost sounded like she was singing the words. Lee adjusted his grip as Xan began to scrape along her nails. The evidence was too valuable to lose to a sudden movement. But she didn't move or even try to pull away.

Lee considered her calm manner. It truly surprised him. Everything he knew about her society said she should be struggling in panic. The Indians were a primitive society.

Chenoa didn't know what to try next. Maybe her English was poorer than she'd believed. Perhaps she'd said the words in the wrong order. Many languages had the verbs and nouns in different orders. She had only practiced English with her own people so maybe they were speaking it incorrectly. "Tell me what you are doing, please."

Xan rolled his eyes up toward Lee and waited. Their patient rolled her head slightly toward them to hear better.

"Do you know where you are?"

Chenoa almost smiled with relief. He did understand her. "No. Who are you, please?"

Xan finished with her hands and Lee laid them on her stomach. She raised one toward her eyes and he stopped it. "Your eyes are burned. They need to stay closed. Understand? Leave the bandage over them."

"Yes, I understand you." Chenoa let her hands rest on her chest. The fabric covering her was hard and her fingers smoothed over it as she tried to decide what was on top of her.

Lee watched her hands. She was really quite resourceful. With her eyes useless she was attempting to discover her surroundings with her remaining senses. It wasn't the wild thrashing of a captured animal, instead she seemed to be mastering her fear and trying to use reason to get the information she wanted.

That behavior didn't fit with the information he had on her culture. On impulse he reached for one of her hands to judge her reaction. She didn't resist. Instead her arm was relaxed as she waited to see what he would do with it.

He was ignoring her question. Chenoa was certain she had said the words correctly this time. But he didn't answer. He held her wrist in the air for some time before he pulled it back toward where he stood. Her hand was placed over some type of container. Tall and round.

"Water." Her hand was settled back onto her chest and she listened to their feet as they left. Chenoa strained her ears for any sound but there was nothing.

Lee moved back toward his terminal and punched in his pass codes. He needed information because what he'd been sent as a briefing on the area must have been wrong. Even in shock, his guest wasn't living up to the image that he'd been given. The Indians were considered hostile, primitive and, most importantly, ignorant.

So exactly why was this one bilingual?

Chapter Three

Morning brought Chenoa relief from much of her agony. Sleep seemed to have chased her body's spasms away. Fatigue was still clinging to her but she reached for the water and sipped at it experimentally. She still wasn't too certain if her body would accept any nourishment, even water.

The water was cool and her mouth eagerly absorbed it. Chenoa had to resist the urge to tip the container up and gulp down the fluid. She took another sip and sat it back on the table.

She had to be careful. There was no telling when or if she would be given more water. Her hands moved to her face and she tugged at the binding that covered her eyes. It came loose and she raised her lids. Pain returned with a burning intensity. Not sharp and unbearable, but the burning was so hot she snapped her eyes closed again.

But it was better than the day before. Chenoa repeated that to herself and tried to build her confidence with the small bit of information. She couldn't lose hope. A positive attitude would be her best hope for returning home.

Sitting up, she ground her teeth together. Her body wasn't cramping any more but it was very sore. Tentatively, she moved her legs off the bed 'til she felt the floor. Standing up, her head swam in a dizzy circle but a deep breath helped ease the sensation away.

There were voices in the distance. Keeping her steps tiny, she held her hands out and moved toward the sound. Maybe she could discover something useful if she listened.

Her fingers found a solid wall and she flattened her palms against it. Bit by bit she moved along its hard surface 'til it opened into a doorway.

Heavy steps hit the floor and came closer. From the sound, it was most likely a man. Chenoa pressed herself flat against the wall and waited. Her bare feet felt the tiny vibrations of the floor as the footsteps came nearer.

Everything stopped and Chenoa felt her heart contract. She strained her ears but nothing moved. But she could feel his eyes on her. It was a distinct rush along her nerve endings as she was studied.

"You shouldn't be up." She knew his voice. The deep tone was rooted inside her head from the night before.

"I am not sick."

Well, she should be. Lee considered his victim with complete uncertainty. He had no idea what to do with her. Every bit of information that he'd dug up on her people didn't support the reality that she was showing him. For a primitive woman she was remarkably poised.

"What place is this?" Chenoa decided to stop using the word please. The two men had not responded to the polite term the night before. Maybe it was considered weak instead of polite.

"Enforcer station." Lee didn't bother to give her the section number. He didn't expect the information to mean anything to her. But her persistence deserved an answer unless he wanted to be downright rude.

She nodded her head and Lee shook his. "You understood that?"

"Yes, I am not ignorant." Chenoa had to control her temper. The man was rather harsh. But she tried to school herself to mildness. He was taking care of her and that was a burden. She should find patience for his surliness.

"Let's hear what you know."

Her temper reared its head anyway. Lifting her head, she decided to meet him head-on. When facing down an arrogant stallion, you had to have a strong show of strength or the animal wouldn't respect you.

"The Enforcement Act of 2176 abolished civilian law agencies and empowered the military branches to unite into the Enforcer ranks. All law-keeping falls under their jurisdiction. May I see the commander of this station?"

"That's me."

She actually snorted. Oh, it was soft and barely audible but Lee distinctly heard the harsh sound. "You have a problem with that?"

"I wish it were not so." And that was the truth. Chenoa refused to be polite to him any longer. He certainly wasn't trying to be helpful so she would stop trying to be nice.

She lifted her chin and pressed her lips into a solid line. Lee felt his lips twitch up. She was actually insulted. Her strength impressed him. Her eyes were swollen almost shut and every inch of flesh not covered by her clothing was scraped and bruised from her abduction. Stepping closer, he stopped when she pulled her breath in sharply. She turned her head toward him.

Enforcers were trained to use all their senses effectively. But his captive was doing it as well. If he were blind he'd be doing exactly what she was doing right now. Lee felt his face set into a deep frown. There was much more to this woman than what he had thought he knew about her.

The side of her jaw was heavily bruised. Lee reached for her face to turn it up to the light. It was time to tend to some of her injuries before all of her wounds became infected.

His fingers made the briefest contact before she smacked his arm away. The blow was quick and efficient. His arm snapped back. Lee glared at her as the spot began to throb but, with her eyes covered, the harsh expression didn't have much effect.

"You should not touch a person without asking for permission." Chenoa felt her composure crumbling. Pain was coursing along her body again and she didn't seem to have the strength of an infant. Her legs were trembling as she tried to stand still. No stranger had ever touched her. There were no strangers on the reservation. His touch drove home the fact that she was so alone.

"My apologies."

She said nothing in response. Instead her head lowered to the wall and she rested against it. Stepping closer, Lee caught the tremor that was shaking her body.

Despair took the last of her confidence and crushed it. Chenoa felt her heart constrict as she lost her fight to stay on her feet. What did it matter anyway? There was nothing here but a man who was a stranger. His opinion should not matter to her.

But not even caring about his opinion left her with nothing but hopelessness.

Lee caught her collapsing body and stood with her cradled against his chest. He wished he had a single clue what to do with her.

Jesus, he hadn't even asked her what her name was. Another shudder shook her body and he smoothed his fingers along her arm. Her hair was a deep, robust brown that held his attention. Stepping toward the cot he settled her onto it. The makeshift bed shook slightly and Lee steadied it.

Brushing her hair out of her face Lee took a moment to inspect the bruise on her jaw. She was out cold so he could touch her now. No, that wasn't very gentlemanly but he was enjoying it. Her skin was a light brown and as soft as cotton. Lee smoothed a hand over her cheek as his lips lifted into a grin. His nostrils flared slightly as he caught her scent. Women could smell clean but Lee had never met one that smelled…attractive.

This one did. The scent seemed purely female and sent his blood pounding toward his staff. Letting his eyes drift down her body he felt that sting of arousal sharpen. She had fuller curves than any woman he knew. Coupled with her scent it made her exceptionally arousing.

Shaking his head, Lee adjusted a jacket over her chest. Too bad she wasn't awake.

He needed to be smacked again.

Chapter Four

Sleep was a wonderful healer. Chenoa found herself as gleeful as a child on Christmas morning when she woke up. Her eyelids lifted to grant her blurry vision. She indulged in a few moments of curious searching around her environment before she closed her eyes again.

The burning was back but not as insistent as the day before. The enforcer commander had instructed her to keep her eyes shut. Chenoa really wasn't inclined to yield to his authority. That didn't mean she was going to be foolish enough to ignore what might possibly be sound advice. No one ever came back from the outside world so she didn't know anything about treating burns that were caused by the fence.

But it stood to reason that an enforcer commander would know such things. In any case, her sight was too great a thing to lose to stubborn pride.

Reaching out for the water container, Chenoa brought it to her lips. It was fresh and cool. Someone had brought her new water today. But there was an unfamiliar taste to it, which she wrinkled her nose at. It did not smell…clean.

Swinging her feet off the cot, Chenoa was careful to stand up slowly. A slow, even breath kept her head steady as she moved toward the doorway again. She wrinkled her nose again. Her body smelled worse than her grandmother's Casmir goats.

Washing was very important to her. She bathed twice a day, everyday. Her skin felt grimy and tight. The desire to bathe battled with her hunger. Both needs were urgent and racing toward a brain that finally felt able to sort out logical thinking again.

A list of tasks ran through her mind as her hands found the doorway. Her frustration doubled as Chenoa considered how useless she would be to her grandmother without her sight. There was no telling how long it was going to take for her eyes to heal.

But her grandmother was very experienced in the art of healing. It was time she found her way back home. She didn't belong here. The enforcers didn't know what to do with her either. She'd been sleeping under their jackets because they just weren't sure where to put her.

Chenoa stepped into the hallway. She needed to find that commander again. Maybe the reason the man was so rude was because he didn't like uninvited guests. He didn't know where she lived so she would tell him and she would be home before noon.

It was slow work making her way down the hallway. The temptation to lift her eyelids was strong. But Chenoa was too worried that she'd do her sight permanent damage if she tried to make her eyes work while they were still so sensitive. With most things, time was important. If you stood on a healing bone too soon it would break again, setting you back at the beginning of the recovery road.

"I'd say you're feeling better." She tilted her head toward him again but this time she lifted her eyelids and tried to look at him. Lee stepped forward and covered them with his hand. It was faster than telling her what to do. He wrapped a hand around her waist to hold her still because any light allowed into her damaged pupils could cause irreversible damage to the corneas.

He was so very strong! Chenoa had never felt such iron strength before. The way he held her body was very powerful and almost dominating. She squirmed against the hold because it agitated her. There was a rush of sensation moving through her body in response. Her skin turned hot and she pushed against his chest to gain distance.

But Chenoa pulled her hands away before he complied with her demand. His chest was coated with more of that same thick muscle that she seemed to notice so keenly. It felt deeper and thicker on the wall of his chest. He even smelled strong.

His scent was very different. Chenoa sniffed at him curiously. Her skin turned hotter and her breath seemed caught in her throat.

"You've got to keep your eyes closed. The bandage was to keep light out. It has to stay on for a week." Lee kept his hand in place and pressed his fingers into a tighter seal. It was suddenly vital to make certain that she healed properly under his supervision. Leaving her alone in the office had been a mistake.

Well, that was going to have to change. She wasn't acting helpless. In fact, Lee couldn't remember if she'd even complained about the pain. He shifted slightly as she squirmed against his hold. Her body felt a little too good next to his as Lee watched her pull her hands away like his chest had burned her. A shiver ran down her back and he smoothed his fingers along her back in response.

"I kept them closed. The bandage was dirty." Chenoa raised her hands and slipped them over her eyes. He let her take over the task and she sighed with relief. Chenoa didn't want him so close to her. It was making her shake. "I was looking for you."

Now that wasn't what Lee was expecting. "Why?"

"I will tell you where I live. My grandmother will tend to me." Just saying the words out loud seemed to make Chenoa long for home even more.

"You won't be going anywhere for a while."

"But why?" Chenoa didn't understand. "You don't want me here. I hear it in your voice. Besides there is no place for me here." Her stomach growled low and deep. It was humiliating that she couldn't even provide her own food. "My family will tend to me. Please send me home. It is my family's duty to look after me."

"Right now, it's my duty." Lee hooked a hand over her arm and pulled her forward. She wasn't expecting the movement and she stumbled. He shook his head and used a gentle pull to move her further.

Lee took her into the kitchen and settled her in a chair. He needed her testimony. That meant he was going to have to make sure she was well enough to give it. The station was stocked with standard field food stock. Pulling one of the insulated pouches from the storage unit, he opened it.

"Here's something to eat. I'll get this worked out a little better. What's your name?"

"Chenoa." Sniffing at the item in her hand, Chenoa pressed her lips together with frustration. The food smelled rotten. Even with her stomach growling, she couldn't force herself to eat it. It stank too badly.

She laid the food aside and Lee frowned. He couldn't send her home. Not yet. In fact it might take weeks to get everything lined up. She had to eat. But the way she used her senses still impressed him. She had sniffed at the food and discarded it. Smell was a very powerful part of a person's taste.

Now an enforcer was trained to eat what was available no matter what their sense of smell told them. But this wasn't one of his men. Some way he had to get her to eat.

Turning back toward the kitchen, Lee searched for anything to give her. Everything in the station was preserved but he doubted she'd eat any of the meals the kitchen was stocked with.

The Indians still grew their own food on the reservation. Lee hadn't seen fresh food in the month since reporting for duty at the isolated outpost. What he'd give for a lousy apple right now himself.

"So, maybe we should start with a shower."

* * * * *

"Sir? I don't think that came through clearly."

Lee rolled his eyes. There wasn't a single speck of static on the communication line. The enforcer recruit on the other end was just too modernized to understand his orders.

"I want two laying hens. As in chickens. Alive." The recruit was heading in from Salsona City and although it was a modern hub of society, there were specialty markets that catered to the extremist's tastes.

"The China sector will have them. I want the birds alive. Clear?"

"Yes, sir." The recruit still didn't have a clue. Lee would be lucky if he didn't get chicken feather pillows delivered to him. Fresh eggs were a delicacy served in only the finest of restaurants. Those birds were going to cost a fortune.

At least the shower was working well. Lee listened to his guest as she moved around in the hot spray of water. Chenoa. He rolled the name around his mouth for a second.

His lips turned down as he considered his success.

Any Indian woman who had been sold into the modern world was not allowed to reenter the reservation. Still uncertain about what caused the sterility, no one wanted to chance infection being spread to one of the few unaffected populations left on the planet.

But he hadn't rescued her until she'd crossed the fence. As long as she stayed on his compound, there wasn't any law that prevented her return to her people. He'd have sent her back already but she was his witness.

Witnesses were sent to protective housing to await trial.

But if he sent Chenoa there, she would never be allowed to reenter the reservation. That twisted his gut. She was foreign to his world but she wasn't what he expected. This wasn't some ignorant savage that would lead a better life in the modern world.

Hell and damnation.

One month in the desert and his brain had fried. There was no other conclusion. Procedure was as clear as the desert morning. Chenoa should be put on that transport and checked into the protective housing. She would adjust to her new life. The enforcer commander at the witness facility would do everything in his power to make that transition a smooth one. Besides she wouldn't have any option but to adjust. Without signed orders, Lee wouldn't let her back onto the reservation.

Well, that's what he should be doing instead of ordering his budget to be spent on chickens.

Lee eyed his communication panel and felt his stomach twist again. The idea left a really nasty taste in his mouth. She was ignorant of the law that would prevent her return to the reservation. It wasn't something the general public knew about. It wouldn't be a chore to get her onto that transport.

But that would make him little better than the scum he had sitting in his holding cell. Maybe the enforcers wouldn't sell Chenoa but there wasn't much waiting for her in the modern world. She wouldn't be able to leave protective custody for fear of being kidnapped. So she'd be imprisoned until she willingly chose a protector. It would be some man with the money to afford a security force and she'd be called his wife. But it wasn't much of a choice when you stopped to consider that she had a family waiting for her on the reservation.

So, his outpost was about to become the proud owner of two chickens.

A pair of knuckles rapped on the door. Lee looked up to find Xan giving him a critical look.

"Do I want to know what you're up to, sir?"

His lieutenant gave him a half grin with his question. "Well, we've been given dispensation to deal with the crisis. I'm dealing with it."

"True enough." Xan lifted a black bag off his shoulder and sat it down next to Lee. "You might find something useful in there. Brenda left a few things behind when she cleared out."

"I'd say thanks but I don't want to stomp on your pride, buddy." Lee was already sorting through the clothing and other female things in the bag. At the moment it was worth gold.

"Don't worry. She wasn't cut out to be an enforcer's wife. That's all."

Xan turned around and left. Lee considered his junior officer and shook his head. While it was encouraged that enforcers marry, it wasn't very practical. Remote outposts had a very negative effect on the mental health of a marriage. Being posted next to the reservation brought a whole new twist to the problem.

Xan's wife hadn't been able to look at the fence and not see the babies that were being born on the other side of it. She'd begun desperate attempts to become pregnant. Experimental medications, sold on the black market, had almost killed her.

Xan had sent her back to the city to get her mind off it. Brenda had sent him divorce papers in return.

But Lee had to admit that he wasn't too sorry about it. Only officers were offered housing in remote locations and that meant there were very few places for him to look for female clothing. Brenda's leftovers were worth a fortune right now. Lee had never even had a live-in girlfriend, so he didn't have a clue what the female of the species used to make themselves presentable to the rest of the world. Not that any knowledge he had might be useful.

Chenoa wasn't like any of his girlfriends.

Well, Brenda's belongings were better than his spare uniforms anyway. There was even a hairbrush in the bag. Walking down the hallway, Lee lightened his step. He had a certain intense curiosity about Chenoa. He wanted to see what she was doing without her hearing him approach. That was a bit of a challenge. Lee felt his lips twitch up into a grin. Chenoa used her senses most effectively. It would be interesting to see if he could sneak up on her.

He stopped at the doorway of his office and almost dropped the bag. She hadn't heard him. She sat in front of the window with nothing but one of the jackets on as she lifted her hair toward the sunlight. She let the strands separate and fall then reached for her hair again and lifted it above her head.

Her bare legs were crossed at the ankles as she stretched them out to counterbalance herself. Firm legs that made his mouth water. Every woman he knew was painfully thin compared to Chenoa. Lee ran his eyes over her legs again and smiled. She looked…feminine. Maybe curvy was the right word. He just knew that he liked it.

Someone cleared their throat and Chenoa frowned. Being blind was getting very tiresome. She dropped her hair and stood up. The sunlight was helping but without an open window it was going to take forever for her hair to dry in the climate-controlled building.

"I brought you some things."

"Thank you, Commander." Chenoa held her hand out and waited. She didn't want to go to him. The commander seemed to affect her oddly. She was hoping the other man would come back to deal with her because the man called Xan didn't make her shake.

"Do you need anything besides food?"

His concern was rather unexpected. Chenoa hugged the bundle he'd given her to her chest and chewed on her lower lip for a moment. He was her only option so she might as well try to be pleasant.

"I would like to go outside."

"Why?"

"I want to dry my hair. The air is too moist in here."

Lee felt his eyes shoot straight to the thick curtain of brown silk that hung down her back. It shone with a rich luster he'd never seen before. Long hair was almost unheard of but there was something about Chenoa's hair that just seemed healthier.

He reached for a lock and let it slip through his fingers. She gasped and jumped back from him.

"Let me guess, I shouldn't touch you without asking first."

"Are the women in your society so open?" Chenoa backed up again and hugged her bundle tighter. He was moving silently. She wasn't sure where he was. That knowledge was extremely unsettling to her nerves. Her skin began to tingle as she considered just where he might decide to touch her next.

"Well, I guess they are." Lee wasn't used to having to ask. When he wanted a woman, it had never been hard to get one into his bed. Even being posted to the reservation hadn't deterred some of his friends from contacting him repeatedly. He liked sex and made sure his partner enjoyed it too. A direct approach was efficient.

Sex wasn't hard to get. Pregnancy was now sought after, so women had sex often in their quest for a child. One of the more common theories was that multiple orgasms would result in ovulation. Sexually transmitted diseases had been wiped out some thirty years before, so there was no reason for sex to be considered risky behavior.

Lee considered her reluctance to engage in a casual touch. Something stirred in response. But he felt his nostrils flare as he caught the smell of her recently cleaned body. This time she didn't smell good. She smelled hot and incredibly sexy. His staff erupted into sensation as he caught sight of her barely covered breasts.

Hell. She didn't have a drop of perfume on or even a speck of make-up but his body was pulsing with need as his eyes wandered over her curves. The arousal was harsh but not one-sided. Lee felt his body surge again as he caught the sharp points of her nipples through the jacket.

"I'll take you outside for a while. Get dressed first."

While it was what she'd asked for, Chenoa still thought his words sounded like an order. The door closed behind him and she placed the bag on the cot and began trying to decide what manner of clothing he'd brought her.

Slipping what she hoped was a dress over her head, Chenoa shrugged. What did it matter anyway? She had already decided she didn't like the man. He didn't like her either. But it looked like they would have to deal with each other until he returned her home.

A quick rap landed on the door before it pushed in. Chenoa caught the step of the commander's boots and turned toward him.

"I'll take you outside."

She didn't say thank you. Instead Chenoa picked up the hairbrush and waited for him to guide her. "How long will it take my eyes to heal?"

"A week." Lee forced his steps to be slow as he took her to the back of the station. The afternoon heat hit them the second they stepped out of the station. "Are you sure you want to stay out here?"

"Yes." Chenoa lifted her neck and stretched out toward the heat. It felt good. The station was over-conditioned and her toes had been cold all day.

"All right, I'll be back in half an hour."

Chenoa pressed her lips together in a pout, but let her displeasure dissipate in the desert heat. Thirty little minutes wasn't nearly long enough. But she certainly wasn't going to waste them being cranky.

Her feet were bare because she hadn't had shoes on when she'd been kidnapped and there were none in the bag. She didn't care. There was some kind of hard surface beneath her feet but there was also the slide of sand on top of it. Slowly inching forward she searched for the edge of the patio.

Reaching the sand with her bare toes made a smile lift her face. Lifting her chin she felt the sun kiss it with hot rays. There was a slight wind, which blew across her cheeks, and Chenoa smiled even more.

She wasn't so far from home after all. With her toes sinking into the hot sand, it suddenly didn't seem impossible to get back to her grandmother's house. What had Nacoma told her—you can do anything if the reason is good enough.

* * * * *

"God, damn it all to hell." Dom stared at the Indian girl and cussed again. The bandage wrapped over her eyes told him everything he needed to know. The transfuser let them into the reservation but anyone not wearing a rubber suit would get their nervous system fried. That worked in their favor because their captives didn't put up much fight while they were blind and puking.

The Boss would want her vaporized. Dom considered his weapon but left the pistol on his belt. Selling human flesh made him a good living and he liked the good life. This little pretty was worth an entire month on an atmosphere cruise. He'd be able to afford one of the penthouse cabins too.

Hell, as plump as her tits were, he'd get enough to cover his gaming. But he couldn't exactly swipe her off the porch of the enforcer station. There was a robotic eye right over the doorway and it was moving with her every step.

Nope. There were already two idiots inside the station's holding cells. Dom wasn't planning on joining them. It would be a lot easier to nab her from a transport. But a couple of his buddies would be needed for that.

Eyeing her tits once again, Dom crawled back across the scrub brush so that he could use his communication unit.

A sadistic smile curled his lips up as his eyes caught the sight of the transport convoy making its way up the desert road.

His pleasure cruise was in the bag.

* * * * *

"I haven't seen a chicken in fifteen years." Xan held the wire cage up and inspected the two birds with a critical eye. "At least not one that was still alive." One of the hens squealed and flapped her wings, making the cage shake.

"Don't scare my chickens, Xan." His lieutenant grinned and licked his chops in suggestion. Lee grabbed the cage while sending his man a sour look.

"Fried chicken or convicted pirates." Xan's face lost all amusement as his eyes burned.

"I should have dropped my weapon out in the field and saved us all a lot of trouble. One misfire would have saved the world the trouble of exterminating those vermin."

It was a rough comment but his men were rough. Xan wouldn't cross the line quite that far but it was still a rather pleasant idea. Selling a human being made them little better than their medieval ancestors. Slavery was inhuman.

Looking past the transport, Lee found his guest. Chenoa was enjoying her time in the sun. She belonged in the desert. She was digging her toes into the sand and stretching her face toward the blazing sun. The dress blew in ripples around her thighs as her hair moved across her back.

Catching the firm cut of her thighs as the wind picked up her dress...well, that was just part of the joy of being a man. The bite of arousal hit him and Lee savored the sensation for a few moments. Women were amazing creatures. Taking one to bed was a clashing of souls that could keep a man sustained during the darkest of endeavors.

As she stretched her neck toward the sun, the smooth column of flesh looked inviting. Lee smiled as he considered her telling him not to touch her without asking.

So, just what exactly would she do, if he asked to taste that lovely neck?

A low laugh rumbled out of his chest in response. Somehow, he couldn't quite picture her saying, "Bite me". Oh, but the possibilities of what could happen if she did.

"So that's how it is." Xan sent him a raised eyebrow and Lee shook his head. "All right." Xan turned a considering look to Chenoa and let his eyes slip down her body.

He and Xan spent too much time together because Lee instantly identified the look on his comrade's face. Lee shoved the chicken and her cage back into his lieutenant's arms. Xan rocked back onto his heels but sent Lee a smirk.

"Take a hike, Lieutenant."

Xan tossed his head back and laughed. Settling the cage in his arms, he turned and started talking to the chicken on his way around the station. "I do believe our good commander is jealous."

"I'm not jealous."

Xan continued talking to the chicken. "Denial makes humans grouchy."

Pulling another case from his transport, Lee opened it and savored the scent of fresh fruit. There was a slim selection of fruit that his recruit had decided would travel well without refrigeration.

Apples and oranges. Some small melons and a grapefruit. Space was tight on the transport and the case was filled to the last millimeter. But two cases and the chickens were the limit. Lee had an entire contingent of men that needed supplies.

Selecting one of the apples, Lee turned toward his guest. He ran a critical eye over her frame and smiled. She was half his size. It was doubtful she ate anywhere near as much as he did.

Chenoa knew the commander's step now. There was a certain rhythm that he walked with. Her ears picked it up and she sighed. Her time must be up.

"I've got something for you." His voice sounded amused. Chenoa wished she could see his face now. This man had very precise opinions. She could hear them in his voice. It would be interesting to discover if she could see them in his eyes. You could tell a person's true feelings when you read their eyes. The eyes did not lie even if the voice sometimes did.

He lifted her hand and left something round behind. Her skin tingled where he'd touched her and Chenoa frowned slightly. Being blind was making her far too sensitive to his touch. She had never noticed that a human touch could make her tremble before.

Her sensitive fingers moved over the apple as she lifted it to her face. Lee found his eyes transfixed with her tiny motions. It was almost erotic the way she used those slim fingers. She sniffed at the apple in a delicate motion before her face lifted into a smile of joy. Her hand began to tremble as her stomach growled low and deep.

"Thank you." She really meant it. Lee watched her open her mouth and use a tiny bite to pierce the skin of the apple. Her tongue appeared and ran over her lips to capture any juice that might be lost.

That same bite of arousal hit him and this time Lee gritted his teeth as it gained force. There was a purity about her that he'd never seen in a woman before. The small act of biting into that apple had to be more enticing than any woman he'd ever seen completely naked.

Suddenly, Lee understood what would make a man pay a fortune for her. It went beyond her fertile uterus. Chenoa was an endless wonder of stimulation. Her very joy of living touched him and made his skin pulse.

Her even teeth appeared and punctured the flesh of the apple again. The control she exerted over her appetite amazed him. She was savoring the food, every bite, and every last drop of juice.

Lee found himself wondering if she would do the same with a lover. His sex rose to stiff attention and he clamped his jaw together in response. Her reluctance to grant him permission suddenly became a challenge that Lee was all too willing to take.

And he never backed down from a challenge.

Chapter Five

Chenoa was driving him insane. Lee was almost positive her scent was causing his brain to devolve. Tossing his shirt aside, Lee left his bed to walk into the dark living room. His housing quarters were small. Two bedrooms attached to a common room, one on either side of that living area. The design offered the most privacy to two officers who might find themselves sharing quarters.

Right now, Chenoa slept in that second bedroom. Lee didn't need to see her. He could smell her. His sex stood at sharp attention as her feminine scent filled his lungs. After sharing quarters with her for nearly a week he was mutating into some primitive animal. The need to get between her thighs burned through his bloodstream constantly now.

He couldn't dismiss it and he didn't want to anymore.

Lee sharpened his eyes as the shadows shifted. It looked like he wasn't the only one who couldn't sleep. Chenoa was still blind. But that didn't seem to stop her from moving around the quarters.

She was at the small sink at the end of the common room. Moonlight spilled over her body making Lee clench his teeth. The dress she wore was thin and all he wanted to do was rip the thing off her body.

Hell, he just didn't understand the intense urges filling his body. But the pulsing tempo held him balanced on the edge of civility. The primitive need to mate was riding him hard.

She turned to show him the tight little buttons of her nipples. They lifted the dress away from her body as she sat a drink glass on the counter. Her bare feet made only slight brushing sounds as she began walking toward her room. But she didn't walk along the wall. Instead she simply walked across the center of the room.

Lee stepped into her path. She held a single hand out in front of her body. Her fingers brushed his chest making his skin tighten. Her scent became stronger.

"Can't you sleep, Chenoa?"

Her belly twisted into a knot. Chenoa felt her breath rattle in her chest too. It was almost as if she'd conjured him up from her imagination. Her mind had teased her with images of this man as she slept.

Yet he was real. Her fingertips rested against that thick muscle again. This time it was bare. Temptation was far too great to ignore. Chenoa lingered over the touch, absorbing the heat of his skin as she drew in a deep breath to find that strength of his.

Maybe the strong temptation was what made it possible to yield your body to a stranger like a competitor. Right then, without her sight, her fingertips transmitted a deep pleasure from their resting spot on his flesh. Chenoa felt her body jump as she gave in to the need to flatten her palm against his chest.

The hard muscle rumbled with his voice. "Go on."

Should she? Chenoa hesitated. His huge hand closed over hers and firmly moved her hand for her. Heat surged through her hand and straight down her arm from the contact. It flowed in a direct line to her belly, where she began to ache for something very intense.

"Come closer to me." Lee watched her shift but waited.

"Why?"

"Don't you want to?"

She did. Chenoa raised her second hand to touch him as she simply enjoyed the contact. It made her body pulse.

Lee wrapped his arm around her waist to pull her forward. A shiver ran down her back as he raised her chin with his hand.

"God, I want to taste you." Lowering his mouth, he caught hers in a gentle touch.

She jerked away from the contact as another tremor shook her frame. Lee followed her and captured her lips again. He traced the delicate surfaces 'til she parted and yielded to his advance.

His arm was solid steel and Chenoa leaned back as her senses erupted. His mouth moved over hers firmly in a motion that made her skin hum with pleasure. His tongue found hers and stroked along its length making her belly twist toward his body. Pleasure came from the touch so she sent her tongue to stroke his and listened to his deep groan of approval.

The kiss changed immediately. His tongue thrust deeply into hers as his arm clamped her against his body. Against her belly his staff burned its thickness through her dress. Fluid eased down her passage as he continued to kiss her. His tongue thrust deeply into her mouth with a hard demand and the blunt proof of his desire nudged her belly, promising more.

She slipped right out of his embrace. She simply bent her knees until she knelt in front of him. One solid thrust from her legs and she jumped lightly away from him as she pushed back to a standing position.

Chenoa held her palm out. Words were lodged somewhere in her throat. But nothing she said would matter. Her only choice was to appeal to his honor. Her body shivered and wailed for her to return to the strength of his embrace.

Instead Chenoa forced her feet to step back. Such overwhelming need wasn't right. She didn't understand the ache in her passage or the fullness of her breasts.

She didn't run. That brought Lee up short. There was something inside him that would have enjoyed chasing her but that delicate palm made him grind his teeth in frustration.

"Until tomorrow then."

"Tomorrow?"

A harsh laugh came from that deep chest. His hand gripped her chin as he stepped close to her once again. Her body quivered as his heat reached out to touch her. He leaned down 'til his lips brushed her ear.

"You taste delicious, honey. Tomorrow, I'll see if I can't convince you to let me taste the rest of you."

* * * * *

His words haunted her the next day as she counted the hours until sunset. Her body seemed to be in complete agreement with his. She wanted to let him kiss more of her. Raising her hand to her mouth, Chenoa gently traced her lips with a finger.

The motion didn't make her belly react. There wasn't any pulsing, only the throb of memory.

She did not belong in this world. That was such a strange idea. It was the same planet, was it not? Such an odd idea that she didn't belong on certain parts of it.

Moving her hands onto the bandage covering her eyes, Chenoa smiled. Later tonight she would see again. She wanted to see him. Her belly did react to that idea. There was the twisting of her muscles as she considered being able to see the man her fingers had delighted in touching.

Rising to her knees she felt for the window. The room was quiet and she wanted to listen to the night. Her grandmother said that the people were not meant to be alone but always together with each other. Life was about sharing.

Was that why she had yearned for the commander last night? Was it her gender seeking his? Chenoa considered her breasts as the nipples began to draw into little points as she thought about their kiss again.

Chenoa pushed the window open, smiling as the cool air rushed across her cheeks. She sat back on her knees and opened her ears. The night was silent. She was disappointed. One of the enforcers must be walking nearby. The animals were silent in precaution.

Her hair was brutally yanked as someone tried to pull her out the open window. Her hands broke the fall as she shoved herself back into the room. Her attacker grunted and another hand grabbed her arm.

Chenoa ripped her bandage away from her eyes and aimed a punch at the blurry form her eyes showed her.

"Bitch! I'm gonna sell you to the meanest bastard I can find." He hissed his words in a low tone as he came through the open window. Chenoa jumped from the bed. She used her elbow to twist into his midsection. The blow stopped him and he sat heavily on the bed.

"Get out, you thieving badger!" Chenoa aimed another punch straight for his chin. Her hand screamed in pain as she hit his jaw. His head swung to the side with her blow and his eyes glowed with rage as he tried to raise his body off the bed.

Her shoulder was grabbed and pulled back as a fist came sailing past her and struck the man square on his chin. This time he tumbled right out the window and dropped in a heap on the ground.

"Chenoa, my dear, you punch like a girl. Remind me to fix that." She pressed her lips into a pout and Lee dropped his onto hers in a hard kiss.

Her mouth exploded with fire and then he was gone. Right out the window after her attacker. Chenoa followed them to the window. Her temper reared its head because she was not some animal to be sold. Any person who thought so needed a good thrashing and she would be happy to do it!

Lee had to hold his temper in check. His professionalism as an enforcer was straining to hold back his desire to smash the insect that had tried to grab Chenoa again.

"You can't touch me, Enforcer."

The pig's eyes glowed with triumph as he said that. Chenoa jumped out of her window as her temper got the better of her.

She aimed another punch at his smirking face and tried to make the blow resemble the commander's more. This time her attacker's head snapped back and he ended up sprawled in the dirt.

"Chenoa dear, you learn fast." Lee felt his face split with a smile as he yanked her off her feet. She wiggled against him as she tried to continue her battle.

"Savage." The pig spat out the label as he sneered at her. Enforcers hauled him to his feet. Chenoa pulled at the arm that encircled her waist but she was bound to the length of the commander's body by his superior strength.

"My people do not sell their daughters. You are like a hyena that would eat its own young. You are the savage creature without honor."

Lee pulled her away because the suspect was an ugly problem that he didn't want her to face anymore. But the reality of the man being on the housing compound indicated a much larger problem then he'd believed they had. This group of pirates was far better organized then he'd suspected. It was going to take some solid strategy to trap them.

"I can walk very well, Commander." Chenoa wiggled again and gained her release. She stepped away from him and stopped. Her eyes didn't fail her. They let her look with complete thoroughness over the man whose voice could make her shake.

She took another step back as she considered how very large he was. While she did not know many men, Chenoa was absolutely certain she had never thought they grew quite so large. His shoulders displayed a strength that must be extreme.

"Hello, Chenoa dear." He used a tone of voice that he'd used in the dark. Her eyes flew to his face to see what his eyes would tell her. She stepped back as she read the promise sitting there. His eyes were gold and brown just like a hawk's.

"I am not a doe."

Lee watched her shift back from him. Her eyes were fluttering over him in rapid movements that betrayed her nervousness. But she lifted her chin when she spoke and pressed her lips into a firm line.

"'Dear' is a term of familiarity. It doesn't mean the animal." She watched his eyes as he spoke. Lee felt another stab of heat hit his body. He let his eyes inspect her body from head to toe to discover the tiny signs of interest.

"Familiarity is improper. It is forward." Chenoa spoke the words too quickly. Her breath seemed to be rushing in and out of her lungs in a hurry and she pulled a deep breath into her lungs and tried to hold it there. Composure seemed to have deserted her. She could almost feel his eyes as they traveled over her body.

She should not be so sensitive to his eyes. Her body was trembling and she rubbed her palms up her bare arms but the skin was not chilled. Instead it was hot, and tingled where he'd touched it.

Those hawk's eyes watched her hands. His mouth formed into a small grin in response. He spread his arm out in a wide gesture that indicated the house.

"Let's go inside to finish this."

Chenoa considered his invitation but hesitated. It was his home. She wasn't sure if entering it again was a wise choice. He seemed too powerful. It was a level of strength she sensed could overpower her if he decided to do that. His intense eyes were watching her and the dark brown hair on his head seemed to make him even more menacing. The way he had shaved most of his hair away made him look like a predator. There was barely a quarter-inch covering his head.

Looking behind her, Chenoa took her first look at the compound. There were long buildings that sat in neat rows off to her right. Men moved around in front of them and light came through the windows. The yard in front of them was lit by large lights held above it on sturdy poles.

Everything was neat and orderly. Each man wore a uniform similar to the commander's. They were black suits that blended into the night, making their bodies difficult to see.

Chenoa suddenly felt odd. All she saw were men. She searched her memory but couldn't remember ever hearing a woman's voice.

"Are there women here?"

"No, the conditions are too harsh."

Chenoa raised amused eyes toward his and Lee felt a surge of pride for her. This was her home and she survived rather well. In fact she loved her desert. Her people thrived in it.

"Your modern women can not be so soft. Not when you are so strong."

Lee enjoyed watching her walk away from him. Her hips swayed in a sultry motion that his eyes drank in. Her little body was pulsing with arousal. He could pick out the signs, yet she tossed them aside, ignoring the signals.

Her purity suddenly made her intensely desirable. That really didn't make a whole lot of sense. An experienced woman was a great partner in bed. Yet there was still something about Chenoa's awkwardness that attracted him. She didn't just toss her dress aside when her nipples beaded with arousal.

He'd never met a single woman of mature age who didn't indulge her sexual impulses.

She was waiting for him inside his house. She had her brown eyes turned toward the door as she considered him again. Lee wiped his face clean because it was clear she was ready for a showdown.

The way his eyes turned hard wasn't encouraging but Chenoa held firmly to her pride. She would never get her answers if she took refuge in cowardice.

"Why am I here?"

Lee pulled a chair away from his table and straddled it. Chenoa was standing by the window watching him with large brown eyes. The determined set of her face impressed him. This girl had a lot of grit.

"Sit down, Chenoa."

She did it reluctantly. Somehow, she'd never noticed that the commander hadn't told her his name. Yet he used hers freely. Maybe that was the custom in his world but it seemed rather one-sided to her. He gave her a nod of approval as she took a seat on the sofa the room offered.

It was a tiny room but his broad shoulders made it seem even smaller.

"The two men who kidnapped you are being held in custody. You have to testify against them."

"How long will that take?"

"A few weeks."

"Must I stay here?" He gave her a hard nod and Chenoa set her teeth into her bottom lip as she considered his words. One week had seemed like an eternity.

"If you don't testify, they'll go free."

Her eyes mirrored her displeasure. She stopped worrying her lip and pressed her lips into a firm line instead.

"They will come back again." Chenoa knew that without a doubt. Nacoma's face flashed before her eyes as she considered that her friend might be the next victim. Suddenly she understood why her attacker had been so confident that the enforcers could not touch him. The pig thought she was a coward and would scurry home leaving him free to rape her people again.

"I will hope that it does not take too long. My grandmother needs me."

Lee felt guilt tug at his plans. The truth was, he still wasn't sure if he was going to return her to the reservation. It might be possible but the truth was, his superiors wouldn't thank him for doing that.

Chenoa would be a welcome addition to the population. Important men would look rather kindly on the enforcer ranks if he turned a fertile woman over to their pursuit. It would be a wise career move on his part.

But she was becoming a lot more than a command decision. Maybe that was due to the fact that he'd been the one to rescue her. Lee really didn't know. But he had a growing desire to see Chenoa remain in her desert.

* * * * *

Her dreams were not kind. Chenoa woke as the horizon was just turning pink and her head ached. She slipped out of her bed anyway. What had she done to turn fate against her anyway? Ever since Nacoma had first begun displaying her rounding belly, everything was just...wrong.

It was so very frustrating. Chenoa watched the sun rise and felt relief flood her. She could see the edges of the clouds turn pink and then to gold and lastly to fluffy white. The desert landscape showed her its different shades of rust and gold mixed with brown and even green.

Maybe she hadn't realized just how frightened she'd been that her eyes wouldn't recover completely. Sight was such a wonderful blessing. Life without it would have been very difficult.

The hens began greeting the morning and Chenoa went to see them. She watched them as they cleaned their nests and flexed their wings.

Lifting the latch on one of the cages, she took one of the birds into her arms. It clucked nervously as she made certain to fold its wings under her arms.

"Good morning." The man named Xan stood watching her with his light-colored eyes. Chenoa smiled as he sent her a wink. He pointed at the hen and shook his head.

"I've never seen anyone actually pet one of those."

Chenoa smoothed her hand over the bird's feathers and listened to her contented clucking. "All creatures enjoy being touched. She will lay larger eggs when she is happy."

"How do you tell when a chicken is happy?"

His tone of voice told her that he thought she was jesting with him. Chenoa considered him a moment. "The people live in harmony with the other creatures on the planet. This hen has as much right to peace as I do."

Chenoa returned the hen to her nest, making certain the latch was secure. She looked at the cage and sighed. She was understanding her grandmother's opinion of the fence more and more these days.

"It's a chicken, Chenoa."

The commander's voice was full of authority this morning. He stood surveying her and Xan with a tight face. Xan gave his commander a hard nod and left. The action struck her as very territorial. She found herself feeling as caged as the hen.

Her temper reared its head again. Chenoa didn't feel like being patient today. "You should not judge me so harshly." His eyes snapped at her and she raised her chin in firm resolution. "I was not misbehaving."

"I'm placing you under protective guard today."

She lifted guarded eyes toward his and frowned. Lee gritted his teeth. He wasn't going to budge on the issue of her safety. It would be done his way.

"You'll need to wear this on your ankle. It's a location beacon."

"I will not be chained like an animal. I have committed no crime. I will not wear it."

She snorted again. Lee considered the small feminine sound and clamped his jaw together. Her eyes noticed his temper but it didn't seem to make a difference. Instead she raised her stubborn chin higher into the morning light.

He struck with the lightning quickness of a snake. One booted foot knocked her feet right out from under her as he caught her falling body in the cradle of his arms. But he didn't hold her, just controlled her landing as he went down on one knee with her. Chenoa was lying on the desert sand before she realized that the commander had pulled one of her legs up in front of her. There was a metallic click and he released her foot.

His large hand caught her chin as she aimed her furious eyes at his face.

"I'm sorry I didn't make it back last night, honey."

Actually he was mad. Lee caught her scent and cursed again. Securing pirates took way too much time and it cost him another night of sleep. He'd stood in the kitchen just waiting for Chenoa to rise from her bed. Instead the woman slipped out the door the second he stepped into his morning shower.

The location ankle bracelet would make sure she didn't become prey to another band of outlaws. "It's a different world out here, Chenoa. Your safety is something I have to ensure."

Chenoa opened her mouth to protest and he sealed the words inside with a hard kiss. His hand held her chin as he thrust his tongue deeply into her mouth. Pleasure shot out from the contact as her hands lifted and sought out his chest. The fabric of his uniform frustrated her. Chenoa thrust her own tongue toward his as she tried to deepen the contact between their bodies. Need pulsed through her passage as he lifted his lips from hers.

"Your escort will be here in a moment."

He turned on his heel and left. Chenoa watched the man climb into one of the large vehicles that they used to move over the desert sand. It sprang into motion the second he sat down and left with a cloud of dust marking its path. Color flooded her face as she considered the smirks sitting on the rest of the commander's men's faces.

Four of the men that had stood near the transport aimed their eyes at her and walked down to where she still sat on the desert floor. All four looked at her before they began to survey the surrounding area. They had their fingers resting on their weapons but their eyes were constantly moving. Over her and over the compound, then back to her.

Chenoa couldn't breathe. She felt more like a captive at that moment than she ever had before in her life. The worst part was, these were the men who were sent to protect her.

Resentment made her angry and she stood up in the face of their presence. She would not bend in front of them.

As soon as the transport disappeared from her sight, Chenoa swung her face back around to her companions. If the commander thought he'd bested her, the man was in for a surprise. Chenoa considered her options.

"Who knows how to throw a punch correctly?"

Their eyes immediately focused onto her face as interest appeared. "Your commander says I punch like a girl." A few dry laughs were her response.

"Maybe you can help me fix this?"

"Lee, I think you may have created a monster." Xan slapped a solid hand onto Lee's back as they pulled into the housing compound. Lee slowly pulled his eyeshades off and watched Chenoa in the evening light.

She was trying to kill one of his men. The enforcer in question had his protective body armor strapped on and was attempting to tackle Chenoa. She responded with a vicious kick to the man's groin. Next, she sent a punch toward his face. Another well-placed knee to the man's chest and he surrendered.

Her shoulders hurt and her chest was heaving but Chenoa raised a proud smile at her guard. The man grinned behind his clear face guard. The grin melted away and he stood up straight. Chenoa turned to regard the commander as he came toward them.

His hawk's eyes considered her as he hooked his hands over his chest and under his arms. She felt like she was being inspected. His eyes made precise movements as they covered her face.

Heat streaked along her face and Chenoa frowned. The night air was cool and there was no reason her face should be hot. The breeze hit her arms to confirm that it was not hot. But the heat spread down her neck and right into her breasts. Chenoa frowned deeper because she had never noticed that her breasts could feel hot. It was if she could feel the blood moving through the soft globes of flesh. They suddenly felt full and sensitive, like the fabric of her dress was too tight.

"Dismissed, gentlemen."

A chorus of "Yes, sirs" hit the evening. The men jogged off across the sand immediately, leaving her to face their commander. But that action pleased her immensely. The ache returned to her belly and Chenoa simply enjoyed it. She didn't want anyone else around. Only the man who made her skin hot.

His eyes changed the second his men's footsteps faded away. They turned completely gold and dropped deliberately to her breasts. Her breath caught in her throat as the sensation doubled. Her nipples rose into hard buttons, which strained against the dress even more. Her skin was begging to be free of the clothing.

His hand came out and gently stroked the side of her face. Chenoa felt her eyes close as the pure pleasure of the touch captured her entire attention. His skin was hot too. His touch seemed to soothe her overheated face. The way his hand smelled was distantly aggressive. Every part of his body radiated his presence to her. Her eyes snapped open as her brain registered the amount of strength his scent seemed to declare.

Chenoa stepped back and shifted as her balance wavered. "You should not touch me." Her voice lacked any conviction. It was a mere whisper because Chenoa liked his touch. The promise he seemed to be declaring was attractive. It awakened a yearning deep inside her belly that twisted tighter with each new sensation.

"Why not, Chenoa?"

"Such touches are not meant to be displayed."

She was too hot with his eyes on her. The heat became worse as it spread to her body and down into her abdomen. A tiny pulse began throbbing in her center.

His huge hand wrapped around her wrist. The grip was solid yet only firm. He turned on a heel and took her with him. Chenoa found her feet hurrying to keep pace with his long legs.

Lee let her go the second the door closed behind him. He walked the few steps to his table to leave his helmet there. He turned to consider the object of his mental dilemma. His skin itched to get out of his uniform. Being in the mood for sex was one thing. This was need and it certainly went deeper than just the intercourse that would relieve his erection. He wanted to touch her, every last bit of her skin, inhale its fragrance as he tasted her.

"Come over here and touch me."

Lee waited to see what she would do. She seemed poised on the edge of fleeing and he wanted to find the means of enticing her closer to him. Capturing her would be simple but tempting her was so much more intense.

Chenoa looked at his huge frame. If she stepped closer he would be even larger, more powerful. The throbbing increased and sank lower inside her body, 'til the folds of her sex seemed too crowded and she shifted her thighs apart to relieve the pressure.

"Try it." Lee extended his hand, palm up to see what she'd do. Her eyes flicked over it and she lifted a slim hand toward him. Victory was swift but she didn't put her hand into his as Lee expected her to. Instead her sensitive fingertips traced over his palm and wrist in a teasing movement that was almost too delicate to feel.

Her fingertips were once again alive with sensation. Chenoa smiled at the pure pleasure she seemed to feel when their bare skin met. Her breasts rose beneath her dress as the nipples drew into tight little buttons.

Lee couldn't remember the last time he'd enjoyed such an innocent touch. He groaned as she ran her hand smoothly over his chest. The strong scent of her body filled his lungs making his body surge forward with the need to take. But having her approach him twisted his senses in an explosion of approval.

Lifting his hand, Lee gently tapped his lips. Her eyes darkened as the tip of her tongue appeared to run over her bottom lip.

"Kiss me, Chenoa."

She wanted to do just that. Wisdom tried to intrude but Chenoa brushed it aside. It simply felt correct to be in contact with him. His body was tense as he held iron control over his flesh. She found herself trusting in this man's ability to temper his strength.

She flattened both hands over his chest before rising onto her toes to comply. Lee clenched his hands into fists as he waited an eternity for that kiss. Her lips were soft as she tried to fit them to his. The contact broke as her toes refused to hold her up. Lee caught her bottom and raised her from the floor. He caught her gasps as his mouth took hers and boldly tasted the sweetness within.

Chenoa twisted as her body seemed to burn from within. She needed to be much closer to him. She sent her tongue searching for his as he turned and she felt the hard surface of the table beneath her bottom. He pressed toward her 'til her thighs parted to allow his hips to settle against her body. The layers of clothing seemed flimsy as the hard bulge of his sex pressed into her most tender flesh.

Yet it filled the ache throbbing there. Chenoa felt her hips thrust forward as pleasure shot deeply into her passage from the pressure. His firm hands slipped up her back before one gently cupped her breast. His thumb rubbed over her nipple making her gasp as pleasure erupted from the little point.

"Commander, sir?"

Lee growled. It was a menacing sound that frightened her with its level of ferocity. He abruptly turned to shield her with his back. The recruit standing in his doorway visibly paled.

"Excuse me, sir... Ah... Command is on the line."

Lee gave a hard nod and the man literally fled. He clenched his hands into fists as the scent of Chenoa's aroused body surrounded him. He couldn't think beyond the need to impale her. It went beyond intoxication. His sex raged with the knowledge that her body was wet and spread for him.

The words that came out of his mouth were vicious.

But he pulled his face into order before turning back around. When he peeled that dress off her shoulders he wanted to spend the entire night between her thighs.

Chenoa pulled her hand back and breathed in slow, even breaths. She lifted her eyes and watched the commander move away. Her mind absorbed the distraction, as her body lamented the growing distance between them. She raised her hand toward her face and caught the scent of the man she'd touched. Mingling with her own scent, it brought the small nub hidden at the top of her sex to her attention as it began to throb with some urgent need. Chenoa suddenly felt very exposed sitting there. She wanted to find someplace to hide and sort out her feelings. She snapped her legs closed before jumping to the floor. His head snapped around to catch her in his sight, making her freeze.

"Chenoa." The way he moved reminded her of a predator and she felt very much like his prey.

"I have to leave again."

He stepped too close and Chenoa shifted away. His hand landed on her hip and curled around it. Chenoa froze with indecision. His hold wasn't steely strong but she knew it could become so. She didn't want him to restrain her. It would be too controlling. So she forced her body to stand still and her nose caught his scent again.

"Go and bathe."

He turned away but stopped and raised an eyebrow as she didn't immediately do as he'd instructed. Instead Chenoa lifted her chin and pressed her lips into a firm line. He nodded his head in the face of her denial and she felt her lips rise up at the corners.

"Until later."

He left on powerful legs and joined his men. Several shapes in the dark moved across the compound in her direction. Chenoa pushed the door closed because she didn't want to be inspected by anyone else tonight. She was too sensitive and her emotions felt drained.

So, she would bathe, but not because the commander instructed her to do it. Pulling her dress off was almost soothing. The fabric had become as abrasive as sand. Looking at her reflection, Chenoa considered her breasts. The nipples were still beaded and hard. But the throbbing sensation had reduced to a mere tingle now. His scent lingered in her memory as she stepped into the water, intending to replace the odd unfamiliar sensations with the common ones of bathing.

Chenoa enjoyed the water of her bath. Her body was stiff from working so hard all day. It was a good ache, which she welcomed. Yet there was also a deeper ache, she considered as she smoothed soap over her torso. It was the oddest feeling. Truthfully, it was a yearning.

Her dress had become a hated thing she was impatient to discard. A slight giggle escaped her. Nacoma would laugh until her eyes sparkled with tears when Chenoa told her about it. The laughter lifted her spirit as she finished her bath with a smile sitting lightly on her mouth.

Duty didn't release Lee 'til the moon was halfway across the sky. His house was dark as he stepped in the front door.

Fatigue might be nipping at his heels but he moved toward Chenoa's room and let his eyes slip over her face.

She'd pushed the window covering aside and lay with the moonlight bathing her face. She'd done something to her hair that kept it tied into a thick rope. Lee didn't like it. Her hair was a dark curtain that he wanted to run his fingers through.

She was so content in her desert. Most people he knew wanted complete darkness when they slept. Chenoa was sleeping as soundly as a child with that moonlight spilling over her face. Her chest rose and fell in deep sleep and Lee turned around.

He wanted her awake when he overpowered her senses. He could stimulate her body right now. She'd be lost in sensation before she even awoke fully but that wasn't enough.

Logic was nagging him with its reasons why he should leave her alone but Lee didn't care anymore.

Chapter Six

Her four guards met her on the front porch at sunrise. They grinned at her. One held up a weapon of some sort.

"The commander says to teach you how to use this today, ma'am."

Although the idea sounded interesting, Chenoa still pressed her lips into a pout.

"That man does enjoy giving orders."

All four men failed to stifle their laughter. Chenoa smiled at them and lifted her chin. It was something to do anyway.

The sun was over her head when Chenoa lowered the weapon to listen to the desert. "What is that?"

"They're opening the fence gate."

"Opening?" Chenoa turned toward the noise and began running. Why had she never considered there was a gate? There must be a way for the competitors to get onto the reservation. She crested the slope and stopped.

Right in front of her the blue field of the fence was gone. Her eyes drank in the view of her peoples' land. Four lines of heavily armed men were in front of the gate. Their rifles were pointed at the gate and another group of men were ordered to leave the reservation.

Some of them did it gratefully. Others lingered. There were people from her tribe standing behind them and Chenoa began running toward the familiar faces. They were still too far away to recognize.

But they were her people.

The blue glow of the fence resumed its function before she made half of the distance. Chenoa stopped in her tracks and felt tears sting her eyes. She just wanted to see them. That was all. She wasn't a coward. She would keep her word but she had wanted to see her home.

"Well. Lookie here."

Chenoa snapped her head around and looked into the face of the competitor who had looked at her that last morning she'd been with Nacoma. His eyes were even more disgusting up close. He looked her over and all she felt was his weakness. His tongue ran over his lips in a vulgar invitation that made her lift her chin with denial.

This man had no honor. Any man who looked at another person as if they were an object was less then human. In his eyes, she felt less important than the dirt beneath her toes. He reached for her body and she jumped back with her eyes flashing at him.

"Do not touch me."

"Come on, you know you want it."

Chenoa forced herself to look into his eyes. She wanted to remember how dirty he made her feel. She could never become so desperate as to enter one of the housing buildings on the reservation. This man was an example of what she would find there. She had seen the proof reflected in Nacoma's eyes.

Her waist was captured in a solid grip that lifted her out of the sand and away from the competitor. Her nose caught the commander's scent but she knew his touch. He set her down and aimed his hawk's eyes at her.

"Do you know him?" The question was a demand. In some primitive way, Chenoa understood that this was not a time to defy the man. If she did, he might decide to fight over her. Confusion hit her in a thick wave because Chenoa was actually pleased that this man wanted to separate her from another male. It was a very dominating idea that her pride battled with. But that did not change what his golden eyes told her.

"I have seen him in the ring." She didn't lower her eyes as she answered. Instead she returned his glare with liquid pools of firm conviction. Lee gave her a hard nod of approval.

The competitors were nothing but a bunch of trained ponies. Lee shifted his eyes onto the line of men he'd just removed from the reservation. They were in prime condition and they wasted it on games. There was too much need for strong men in the world today. While these men might have strong bodies they were indulgent brats inside their minds. They didn't give a damn about anyone but themselves.

They could be firefighters, enforcers or any of twenty other strength-requiring professions. Instead they pushed each other around in the dirt while sticking their penises out like a piece of bait on a fish hook.

Chenoa felt her heart constrict as she looked into the commander's face. He was a strong man. The strength that she felt radiate from him came from his honor and his dedication.

"Why do your people send such poor examples onto the reservation?" She whispered the question because it was born of her endless hours of struggle over whether to look to the ring for a child. How could she have known that right outside the fence were men whose children she would have gladly borne?

But these men did not come to her people. Instead they sent their trash. The slight was unmistakable. The commander and his men didn't think an Indian was worthy of their seed.

She turned on her heel and left. Her eyes had shut him out in a firm motion. Lee didn't know why but he sure as hell meant to find out.

Her bath didn't soothe her today. Instead it just made her skin more sensitive and tight. Chenoa snorted with frustration as her hair tangled and caught in snarls on the brush. She pulled her dress on and shifted in agitation as the fabric scratched her sensitive skin.

She should not care!

The commander had not even told her his name. Yet she liked his jealous display. Pulling her hair over her shoulder she began braiding it to get it out of her face.

Being angry with the man was certainly easier to understand.

"Why are you doing that to your hair?" Lee knew his voice was hard and he tried to soften it. He didn't want to scare her. His body was tense with arousal, straining his control to its limit.

"I just want it out of my face. It is too hot today." Chenoa tossed her finished braid over her shoulder. Her eyes captured the sight of his frame and she snorted again. He was so powerful. Trained and sculpted into a hunter. His black uniform molded to his shoulders to display the muscles to perfection. The small row of insignias that sat on his collar just made him more attractive because this man dedicated himself to something more than his own pleasure.

It wasn't hot. At least not in relation to the normal desert heat. The sun was sinking into the horizon and the breeze had picked up. Lee considered the blush sitting on Chenoa's cheeks and watched her eyes roam over him.

She was aroused. Lee felt his chest expand in a deep breath as he clamped down on his reaction to that bit of information. Her nipples stabbed against her dress as she shifted around on nervous steps. Her face was scarlet with a blush and his sex rose to throbbing attention in response.

"Did you go to him?"

Chenoa raised her eyes to his with angry pride. "I would never bare my breasts for a creature like that. His heart was filled with nothing but selfishness."

"Would you bare them for me?"

Her eyes became large and liquid. Her lips parted in the slightest of gasps before the tip of her tongue appeared to moisten them.

Chenoa knew that she would. The desire to comply with his request sprang up from somewhere deep inside her body. The way he held his position made that desire become a demand. This man wouldn't simply take. He wanted to share the intimacies of the flesh.

But first he wanted her to surrender.

Her eyes dropped down his body again and settled on the bulge of his sex. It was thick and large, pressing against his clothing, just like her breasts were.

"You told me to ask, Chenoa. Aren't you going to answer me?"

He moved forward on those powerful legs and Chenoa felt herself move back. He stopped and laid a large hand over the surface of her cheek. The contact soothed her flesh as she rubbed her face against his hand.

Chenoa savored every feeling. Lee's eyes were glued to the way she absorbed the simple touch of hand to cheek. He pulled his hand back and watched her lift her eyelids. The deep brown of her eyes was a simmering pool of liquid heat that made his body heat double.

"Yes, I will bare my breasts for you."

Chenoa felt her feet leave the ground in a flowing movement. His arms slid over her body, confining her in the solid clasp of his embrace. His possession of her was so complete, Chenoa felt a small ripple of fear travel along her skin. But, she had given him permission. The words were final. His eyes were alight with victory and almost glowed with triumph.

He moved his hands over her bottom, pressing her forward until his erection found her softness. The layers of clothing between them were harsh. Chenoa gently pushed him away. His arms hesitated before releasing her. In her center she knew it was a temporary concession. His control was stretched almost to the limit. This was not a man who let others lead him often.

Chenoa pulled the dress from her body and smiled with relief. Her bare skin rejoiced in its freedom. That same twist of fear came back as his eyes surveyed her. She held her head high as he let those sharp eyes linger over her nude body. Approval covered his face, making her pride surface. He liked what he saw and that pleased her immensely.

His arms closed around her and pulled her into contact with his frame then leaned down and dropped his mouth onto hers again. Chenoa simply moaned, as the pleasure seemed to spike straight through her.

Lee taught her lips the motion and savored her eagerness to taste him deeper. Her innocence amazed him but it made her even more potent. He handled her with iron control. He was going to taste every last inch of her sweet flesh before he gave in to the need to mate with her.

"Open your mouth for me." His lips covered hers as the tip of his tongue traced the line of her mouth. Chenoa let him push past her lips into the center of her mouth. He thrust his tongue deeply into her mouth, demanding compliance. A soft moan escaped her as he stroked her tongue, enticing it to return the touch. Hunger speared through her like a flame of fire. Twisting her head she thrust her tongue forward into his mouth to explore him just as he'd invaded her.

Hooking an arm under her knees, Lee crossed the dark room, kicking his door shut behind them. He left her in the middle of his bed as he yanked his uniform off and tossed it onto a chair. Chenoa rose onto her knees, watching his movements with curiosity.

His bare chest fascinated her. She had guessed he might be powerful but the reality was stunning. She lifted her hands to lay them on the muscles of his chest and felt that same tremor ripple along her skin. His breath was rough as he stood for her touch, his skin hot under her fingertips. A deep mat of hair covered him from his shoulders to his flat waist. Pushing her finger through the strands, she smiled as he growled in a low tone.

"Your touch is amazing, Chenoa."

"I like the way you feel, Commander."

Lee frowned deeply; he didn't like her using his title here. Right here, they were simply humans, not locked in the battle of the planet's survival. The way she touched him was as old as time and the way he wanted to touch her in return was pulsing through his brain on a primitive level that had nothing to do with the enforcer ranks.

"My name is Lee." He rolled onto the bed and pulled her body with his, pressing her into the mattress, holding her there. Her breasts thrust high and proud and he dropped his head to them. Pulling one nipple into his mouth he sucked gently on it. Cupping the soft mound, Lee lifted the nipple further before the tip of his tongue traced the beaded nipple around its peak in a lazy circle that wrung a moan from her throat.

She couldn't contain the tiny sound. His mouth was hot and searing as it pulled on her breast. His tongue rubbed and flicked over her nipple in a motion that set the folds of her sex quivering. The little nub hidden inside them tightened until it ached. His fingers cupped and kneaded her breast making the sensation turn into a wave that engulfed her entire body.

The hair that covered his body was rough. It seemed to emphasize how very male he was. Chenoa threaded her fingers through it as his mouth traveled to her other breast. Her fingers found his nipples and rolled the small nubs between her fingers. His sharp intake of breath made her bold and she rolled the flesh again as her hips thrust forward into him.

His hand immediately moved over the mound of her sex and gripped it. Chenoa gasped. It was a full sound born of pure sensation. He raised his head and caught her eyes in the dark.

Lee held her still and searched her face. Innocence was written across her face but she wasn't frightened. He held her eyes as he deliberately sent a single finger to part the folds of her sex. Her nostrils flared as her chest rose in agitation but he stroked her flesh with that finger and felt the smooth fluid of her desire coat his hand. Lee adjusted his grip and rubbed along her cleft again watching her face for the right touch.

Heat exploded along her body and Chenoa let her eyes fall closed. The throbbing inside her center became a roaring tempo that centered under his hand. Her hips thrust up in tiny motions that she was powerless to control. Instead she surrendered to his touch as he dictated the intensity of the sensation his fingers produced.

Her voice caught in a harsh moan as the tempo reached its crescendo. Her body drew taut as everything centered under his hand. She twisted under the strain 'til her hips bucked and lifted and her body shattered into a moment of pure pleasure. She fell limply back to the bed as she let the ripples of delight wash over her body. Lee dropped his mouth to the satin of her neck, gently nipping the skin as her chest rose in small agitated breaths.

"That was…" Chenoa didn't know how to describe the feeling.

"That was just the beginning." Lee rolled over her body and settled his hips between her thighs. She wrapped her legs around his hips in instinct and his own arousal surged in response. The tip of his sex nudged the wet folds of her body and his hips pushed forward. The meager amounts of control he still had were stretched thin as Lee kept his hips from ramming his erection into her body with a hard thrust. Instead he moved into her with steady strength, which allowed him to feel her body stretching to accommodate him.

The moonlight shimmered off the tiny tears that escaped her eyes. Lee caught them with his fingers. Her passage was so damn tight around him as the flesh tried to stretch around his length. Two more tears slipped from her eyes as he firmly held his body in place. She would take him. His need to be inside her surpassed simple urgency as the realization of her virginity hit him. She wasn't just his, she was *only* his.

A low growl escaped his lips as his hips began to move in the rhythm his body demanded. He cupped the cheeks of her bottom and raised her to meet the demand. Her eyelids lifted as she boldly watched his possession, her body trying to keep pace with his and learning the rhythm that nature designed. Her eyes flew open as she clasped him between her thighs.

"Please, Lee... Faster."

Her body ached and she raised her hips again almost frantically as the motion stroked her swollen nub making it scream with need. Chenoa gripped his arms and felt his strength move beneath the skin. His hips moved in solid thrusts that became deeper and harder as his breath became harsh.

"Jesus, Chenoa, I can't stop."

His body drew as taut as a bow as he rammed his sex into her body. Her own body became tense as sensation crested over her again. Her breasts thrust high as she lifted her bottom for even deeper penetration. Soft and wet, her body took the hard thrust of his as he watched the bounce of her bare breasts beneath him. She gasped as pleasure swept over her again and the soft passage contracted around his length. His cock jerked as it erupted inside her. He rammed his length inside her to the hilt as his seed hit the deepest part of her body. Pleasure slammed into his brain as her passage tightened and milked his cock of every last drop. Lee collapsed onto her as they both struggled for breath. He brushed at her eyes but they were free from tears now. Instead she rubbed her cheek against his hand as she delicately sniffed at his hands.

"Are you all right, Chenoa?"

His voice was rough. Chenoa smiled as she looked into his face. She had made him sound discomposed and that gave her a sense of pride. "Why wouldn't I be well? I am not a child that is too young for a man's attentions. I came of age four years ago."

"So why am I the first man who's done anything with your adulthood?" Lee kept his words low to hide the intense surge of emotion that ripped through him. He didn't have the right to demand anything from her but he was going to understand her.

She shifted in agitation and Lee frowned. Rolling off her body he pulled her into an embrace as he used a firm hand to cup her cheek and raise her eyes up for his inspection.

"Answer the question."

Chenoa shook her head and wiggled away instead. She rose to her knees to consider her partner. The man was too used to giving orders. "I am not one of your men. I will not obey your commands when the matter is personal."

Lee propped himself up on an elbow. She sat poised and straight as the moonlight bathed her nude body. She didn't shirk or try to hide. It frankly amazed him, her complete and total acceptance of their nudity. "Explain that, Chenoa."

"A woman must choose carefully who she lets into her body."

"Sex is normal and healthy, there are no side effects. Sixteen is plenty old enough for a female to begin sharing intimate relations. " His answer was gruff.

"My body is mine to share. Yet on the Peoples' land a girl is not allowed this intimacy 'til she is eighteen and fully mature."

"Eighteen?"

"Sixteen is too tender an age. The body has not yet widened at the hips."

"What's that got to do with sex?"

Chenoa stared at him like he'd lost his mind. Lee watched confusion tighten her face as she tried to think.

"You are unhappy that I have not practiced more?"

"Hell no!" She jumped as he came up off the bed with those words. The idea that anyone would even try to get between her thighs enraged him. Lee didn't stop to think why that was. He caught her waist and smoothed her into his embrace.

A firm hand traveled up her body to cup a breast as she felt the staff of his sex thicken against her thigh. Chenoa was too tired to wonder about his words any longer.

"I will be happy to help you get all the practice you want." She shifted again as Lee frowned. The tears he'd wrung from her as he took her innocence told him to let her rest for tonight.

"Settle down, honey." He tipped her chin up as her eyes shimmered in the moonlight. "You'll be sleeping here."

The firm note in his voice made her shiver. His large hand rubbed along her back as his body curved around hers. His scent filled her senses as her body refused to resist the need to sleep.

Chenoa had never answered his question. Lee remembered that as he stood watching her sleep the next morning. How in the hell did a woman stay a virgin for four years? His mind was having the devil's time grasping that idea.

Four years?

What was she, a nun? His memory was clear and fresh this morning. Chenoa wasn't a nun. But she had been innocent. He'd never suspected she might be a virgin. Women discarded their virginity the second the law allowed it. They marked it on their calendars and made arrangements for their sixteenth birthdays.

But if the age of consent was eighteen in her world then she was twenty-two years old. An amazing age to reach as a virgin. Deflowering innocence was something only boys got the chance to experience. Lee stroked the satin of one cheek before he let his lips curl back into a grin. Deep satisfaction radiated from the knowledge that he'd been the man to take her virginity. All he wanted to do was roll her onto her back and sink back into the newly explored depths of her body.

Leaving the room on silent steps, Lee resigned himself to waiting. She needed her rest.

Chenoa's discarded dress lay over a kitchen chair. Picking up the garment, Lee caught her unmistakable scent. She'd taken it off for him but not for anyone else in four long years? Actually, she'd bared her breasts for him. Lee looked back at the bedroom door. His cock rose to stiff attention as he felt his lips curl up once again. She'd bared those stunning breasts for him and only him.

His boots felt nailed to the floor as he tried to leave before riding her until she moaned once again for him.

Why hadn't he noticed how long a day was before?

* * * * *

She woke up alone in the house again. Chenoa frowned and looked at the midmorning sun. Her eyes grew large and round and she sat up with guilt. No wonder she was alone. It was well past the time to have left the bed.

The commander wasn't a lazy man.

Lee, his name was Lee. Chenoa stepped out of the bed and froze as her body protested her movements. She moved again on slower steps, wincing slightly. Lee was such a large man. It stood to reason that her body would be sore. Chenoa looked back at the bed and considered her actions.

Confusion wrapped around her as she looked at the stain of her own blood on the sheets. There had been so many emotions pulsing through her last night. She wasn't exactly sure what they were. But they had been strong enough to make her yield her trust to a man whose name she hadn't known.

She wasn't sorry. Chenoa lifted her chin and walked toward the shower. She was a woman, fully grown. There was no reason to be innocent any longer. She truly needed to stop worrying about things so much.

Soon, she would go home. Her face lifted because she would not go home without knowing Lee's touch. Maybe fate was guiding her. What a blessing it would be to take Lee's child home to her grandmother.

Her face froze as she considered a child. Lee was not a man who would let her take his seed from his family. Chenoa felt her hands begin to shake because she had never thought about a child last night. Or any of the decisions that went along with becoming a mother.

Her grandmother had tried to teach her the importance of such decisions. Chenoa felt disapproval sitting heavy on her shoulders.

How could she separate a child from such a good example for a father? But she couldn't stay here. She had to go home.

And Chenoa absolutely knew that Lee wouldn't leave his world to join her on the reservation.

They were from two very different worlds. She should not have been so impulsive. Her grandmother's voice floated across her memory in reprimand.

Only bare your breasts for the man that will walk beside you.

But she had wanted to bare them for Lee. Despite her horror about the days to come, Chenoa wasn't sorry. She was drawn to the man. It was such an intense beckoning that she could not have ignored it.

But now she would have to find a way to stop.

* * * * *

"Commander, I've heard a very interesting rumor."

Lee considered his superior as the communication screen let the two men talk over a thousand miles of desert sand.

"I'm sorry to hear you're bored enough to listen to rumors, sir."

"Cute." Russell sat forward and peered into the screen. "Congratulations. I'm going to personally file the case charges today and get this one moving fast. When will you transport the victim?"

"I'm not. She can testify from here."

"You didn't tell me the desert heat was effecting your judgment, Lee."

Lee squared his shoulders and tightened his face. "She wants to go home, Russell. And I do mean home. She's got family on the reservation. Technically, she can be returned if she stays here."

Lee heard Russell snort over the communications line. "That won't make you any friends, Lee."

"Figured that out on my own. But I'm not out here to do things the way they've been done for the past five years. You wanted the job done. I'm doing it."

Russell's voice changed immediately to one of acceptance. "All right. That point will buy you some time."

Russell's warning didn't bother Lee. A man could do a lot if he had the time. Every strategy he knew held the key ingredient of time. He needed to find the ringleader of these pirates. They would continue to come back as long as they had customers.

The money was the key. It was frankly amazing what some people were willing to do to get it. This bunch of scum was willing to vaporize living beings. Yet, their customers were still lining up at the market for fresh meat.

Lee considered his prey as he decided on a trap. Any trap ever built needed to be complete. Lee was sitting on the source but he needed to come up from behind in order to catch the butcher with his hands on the meat.

What Lee needed was a customer to place an order with the black market.

"Xan, exactly how much dealing did your wife do with the black market?"

His lieutenant swung around from his desk and aimed angry eyes at his commander. Lee lifted an eyebrow as he waited for the answer.

"Considering what she managed to buy, I'd say she got in pretty deep."

Lee felt his face set into a hard mask. Brenda had somehow gotten her hands onto an ovulation drug known as suptriproholine. It caused her ovaries to ovulate all right, to the point that her fallopian tubes had burst. She'd almost bled to death before Xan figured out her body cavity was filled with her own blood.

Lee didn't understand that level of desperation. Maybe he just hadn't really taken a close look at the realities of never having a child of his own. Chenoa's face swam before his eyes as Lee considered her giving him a child.

Brenda's decision suddenly became much easier to understand.

"What's on your mind, sir?" Xan didn't like the personal question but it was a credit to their friendship that the man was willing to answer it.

"Think Brenda could place an order for an Indian breeder?"

"Not on my income."

Lee grinned as Xan returned the expression. Setting a trap took patience but both men enjoyed the tension. Outsmarting their opponents held its own rewards.

"So, exactly how do we have Brenda come into a small fortune, sir?"

"You get her to sign on and I'll find the money source."

Lee punched his pass code into his computer as he began searching for a very elusive buddy of his.

* * * * *

Dom was getting nervous.

They'd moved the cunt right into the middle of the housing unit. How the hell was he gonna get her now? Maybe it was time to pack a bag and disappear.

Yeah... It might be a whole lot healthier to just skip the continent. Everything was about to explode.

But that pleasure cruise was just sitting in his head singing out his name. Zeik would have him vaporized in a second if he found out he was gonna skip but black market business carried the same law as the sea.

Every man for himself.

Still... He'd been outsmarting these enforcer jerks for five years now. Seemed really stupid to walk away from a deal like that. One cunt wasn't worth scrapping the entire operation.

It was worth another stab. Besides, the boss man wasn't hollering for him to leave yet. Dom watched the compound with beady eyes. What he needed was to rock the boat enough to make all the enforcer rats scurry.

Yeah... That's just what he needed to do.

A loud crack of thunder made Dom yelp in surprise. The afternoon was dark as a thunderstorm made its timely appearance. Rain poured down on his head a second later as he frantically ran for cover.

The thunderstorm didn't send Chenoa running for cover. Instead, she moved further into the open and stretched her arms toward the heavens. Laughter bubbled out of her chest as the rain soaked her. The water slid along her body, making her feel as clean as a newborn.

Hope seemed to cover her with the rain. Her cares just melted away as she twirled about in complete freedom. Sometimes, you needed to let Mother Earth have her way.

When it rained, get wet. When a man's scent made your blood sing, embrace him. If his seed took root in her womb, be content. Chenoa turned around again as thunder shook the earth under her bare feet.

Lee jerked her right out of her steps. She fell into his body as her eyes snapped open with surprise.

"Go into the house." He bit each word out in a low snarl. Chenoa remembered the tone from the day before when he'd confronted her about the competitor. His eyes were flashing angry fire at her. Chenoa raised her chin in the face of his temper. She caught her escort watching them with vivid eyes, so she turned on her heel and walked toward the house with her lips pressed into a firm line.

It would appear the commander was feeling authoritarian. Chenoa didn't feel like swallowing it again. He hooked her arm, spinning her around a bare second after they crossed into the house. Chenoa brutally shoved his body away from hers. Surprise lit his golden eyes as she stepped further away from him. "You will not touch me," she declared firmly.

Lee felt his temper double. He might be mad as hell at her but there was no way she would put that wall between them again. "You gave me permission, Chenoa." Lee stalked her with each careful word until she bumped into the table. He caught her stubborn chin in a firm hold as he aimed his glare into her eyes. "I will touch you whenever I want to."

Chenoa stomped on his foot. She used her heel but Lee suspected the attack hurt her more than him because of his boots. Catching her waist with his arm he simply pulled her off her feet and sat her on the table to prevent her from hurting herself further.

"You do not have permission to touch me with anger." Chenoa pressed her lips together tighter because she felt them begin to tremble with her hurt. "That is a shameful thing."

Lee nodded his head with satisfaction. "You will not push me away, Chenoa." A warm hand lifted her chin so that his golden stare could capture her eyes. Chenoa felt a shiver pass along her body. Even though she was hurt by his words, her body still sensed his strength and craved it. The arm chaining her to his body immediately began to stroke her back in response to her shivers. It was the unconscious concern of a mate.

"I would never raise my hand to you, honey." His words were bit out again. Chenoa distinctly heard his injured pride speaking. No warrior of honor would ever lose his control with a female. Lee was insulted that she'd thought he would do such a thing.

"Then I do not understand you. You treat me like a misbehaving child once more."

A low growl escaped his throat. Lee watched her dark eyes widen slightly in response. He deliberately stroked her cheek before stepping back to cross his arms over his chest. "There are certain orders I give that ensure your safety. You are my responsibility, Chenoa. I won't have you placing yourself at risk. Is that clear?"

Her eyes mirrored her racing thoughts as his words soaked into her. Lee let her think about it a moment. He was absolutely certain she'd scared five years off his lifespan by dancing in the rain in a transparent dress with a couple hundred raw men watching her.

Chenoa considered the black strap that still clung to her ankle. Her memory was crystal clear as she thought about the morning Lee had forced her to don it. She suddenly understood that he had not been angry at her but with her ignorance of the need for the device.

Maybe she still didn't exactly understand the reason for such measures but Chenoa did realize that this was not a man who left details unfinished. "I still do not understand why you are cross now."

Lee found himself becoming exasperated. "Look at your dress, honey." The thin cotton was clinging to her body showing off her breasts with a mouth-watering effect. Lee pressed his hands flat against his ribs as he tried to think about something besides her tight little nipples.

"It is all I have to wear." Chenoa felt like the words were ridiculous. The only other garment she had was a shirt and she'd been sleeping in it until last night.

"It's wet."

His jaw was clenched tight but for the life of her, Chenoa couldn't understand the man's mood. Truly, she did not understand men. "It is raining."

"Jesus Christ! I know it's raining." Lee couldn't believe they were having this conversation. "You might as well be naked."

Chenoa suddenly laughed. It was low and sweet. She watched the commander's face tighten and she tried to control her amusement. But it was so very difficult.

"My grandmother told me modern women are afraid of their bodies but I did not think it was true." She stood up and began unfastening the buttons that ran down the front of the dress. Lee couldn't help but watch her fingers as she undid each one. "My body is exactly like every other female. Clothes can be useful but they are not needed as a shield. Somehow, I doubt there is any man within your command who does not know what a female looks like beneath her clothing. Do you mean to tell me that your men are not men of honor?"

She dropped the dress over the table and simply stood there to prove her point. She was absolutely magnificent. It wasn't boldness. Instead Chenoa was simply content with herself. She was at peace with her surroundings. Lee felt his gut twist as he considered how his world would exploit her delicate innocence. He felt like he was trying to tell Eve to beware of serpents.

By teaching her, he would be lifting her eyes to look at evil for the very first time.

"Some of my men haven't seen a woman in six months. Much less a naked one." Lee felt heat stab straight through his body as his eyes dropped to her bare breasts. "You wouldn't want one of them to think you were baring your breasts for him."

Understanding crossed her face and Lee moved forward as he cupped one of her breasts. She shivered as he rolled the nipple with his fingers.

Chenoa felt the same mixture of anger and pleasure as Lee made his reasons clear. The man was very possessive of her. Maybe all males were so. It chafed her slightly, yet she couldn't deny the curl of excitement it sent through her belly. He would not share her. It was a very primitive thing that touched her on an equally primitive level.

She pulled his scent into her nose and savored the aggression in it. Her breasts lifted as her body became warm. Chenoa felt her breath come in short pants as she rolled his scent around her head. His fingers firmly pinched her nipple and her eyes flew open to be snared by his glare.

"Kiss me." He was ordering her again but Chenoa felt her blood grow hotter in response. Her sex was throbbing as she considered what else he might demand of her. His golden stare said he wanted complete possession of her.

A naughty little smile lifted her lips before she complied with his demand. But she didn't kiss his mouth. Instead Chenoa lifted his hand away from her breast and rained tiny kisses over it. His breath caught with a harsh sound and she smiled again. Using her tongue she made a lazy circle on the inside of his palm. A hard sound came from his throat before he used both hands to grip her waist. Chenoa found herself seated back on the table as he spread her legs apart with his body. Her hands settled on his chest as one huge hand cupped her head to raise it up.

He kissed her with a raging need. It was hard and steady as he took her mouth and moved it exactly the way he wanted. His tongue thrust inside to taste her flesh.

Tangling her fingers in his hair Chenoa softly moaned as her skin became increasingly sensitive. The fabric of his uniform scratched her pulsing nerve endings. The bulge of his sex further taunted her as it was separated from the folds of her sex by yet more clothing.

Ripping her mouth away from his hungry one, Chenoa issued her own order. "Take it off."

Lee threw his head back and laughed. She wanted him. Plain, simple and without games. But it wasn't sex. Pulling his uniform off, Lee watched her eyes deepen into pools of liquid heat. He noticed all the tiny details of her body, as it demanded his touch. Somehow he knew this was more than just sex. He didn't just want to ride her, he needed to touch her. Hear her moan with the pleasure that he wrung from her body.

He captured a nipple between his lips the second he tossed his pants to the floor. Chenoa felt her breath lodge in her chest as heat snaked straight toward her sex as he pulled and sucked on the beaded tip. His tongue flicked over it and she let her head fall back as pure sensation took control. Her hand twisted in his hair as she moaned.

Moving to her opposite breast, Lee took his sweet time enjoying her body. She smelled exciting and tasted even better. His staff throbbed almost painfully and he enjoyed the bite. In a

Mary Wine

primitive way, he wanted to dominate her body. Bring her arousal to an intense pitch while he watched her.

Releasing her nipple he pressed a kiss to her belly as he lowered himself to his knees. Chenoa opened her eyes to look at him. She wasn't sure what the man was doing. He gently smoothed a hand over her bare mound before his tongue flicked out to stroke her moist center. Sharp sensation stabbed through her and she jerked away from him. But his hands firmly gripped her bottom and pulled her forward toward his mouth. His wide shoulders pushed her thighs open, leaving her tender flesh exposed. This time he sucked part of her flesh right into his mouth. She collapsed onto the table as her body exploded with pleasure.

Harsh and raw, Chenoa was a captive to the spikes of pleasure his mouth drew from her body. He pulled on her sex 'til she ground her hips into his mouth for more. But he released his hold on her and sent his tongue on long strokes over her sex 'til he reached the opening to her passage. She throbbed harder as he flicked around her opening then back toward her center. Her hips thrust up with impatience and she heard his low laugh.

This time he used his tongue on the very center of her body. She drew as taut as a bow as her hips frantically pressed toward the pressure. He pulled the entire nub into his mouth and sucked as pleasure ripped through her center.

Her body lay sprawled across the table. Lee felt himself flood with satisfaction. Standing over her, he watched her heart beat a hard pace against her ribs as she pulled little gasps into her lungs. Cupping her breasts again, he gently rubbed them as she snapped her eyes open to watch him. Her pleasure was reflected in her eyes and Lee felt his body erupt into ferocious pride.

Satisfaction was written across her face and he'd been the one to place it there. Rolling her nipples between his fingers he grinned as hunger crossed her eyes again. Lee let the tip of his staff nudge the swollen folds of her sex. Her chest lifted with deep breaths as she opened her legs wider for him.

His thrust was hard. Chenoa arched her back to absorb it. Her body remembered the way to hold him as he rode her with a hard rhythm that made her gasp. His eyes bored into hers as his body possessed her. She began to grow tight again and her eyes slipped closed as sensation centered around his thrusts.

"Look at me, Chenoa." His voice was as hard as his body and she opened her eyes to see him clenching his jaw against his own release. The harsh cut of his face grew taut as her hips pushed frantically toward his thrusts. Pleasure spiked through her a second before he drove into her body and let out a load groan. Their combined pleasure seemed to feed off one another as he braced his weight on his elbows just an inch above her body.

Lee brushed her mouth with a warm kiss then his hands cupped the sides of her face as he lingered over her mouth in a soft kiss that stretched on. His hand smoothed over her back before lifting her off the table. "Let's find something softer for you to lay on, honey."

Chapter Seven

Lee's bed was certainly softer but Chenoa looked at the table rather fondly the next morning. She giggled lightly as she found her dress flung over a chair. Lee must have taken the time to arrange it there before he left because she certainly hadn't given any attention to the task last night.

Her smile faded and Chenoa shook her head. She did not understand him sometimes. Pulling the dress over her shoulders, she sent the buttons into their holes with quick movements. The dress was only half dry and rather uncomfortable. A morning walk would dry it though.

Chenoa felt her laughter return as she considered just what Lee might think of her sunbathing. A body was a body. She couldn't count the times she and Nacoma had tossed their clothes aside to play in the well water when the sun was mercilessly hot. While Nacoma might have larger breasts than Chenoa did, they were still only breasts.

But Lee did things to them that Chenoa had never heard of. She smoothed her fingers over the cones of her breasts yet didn't feel the intense heat that Lee's hands transferred. Instead, she was simply reminded of the feel of bathing herself. It certainly wasn't exciting.

Yet when Lee touched her, it was more than exciting. There was a violence to the sensation that made her think of yesterday's thunderstorm. Yes, Lee affected her very much the same way the storm touched the earth, completely consuming until both were spent.

Her body ached again this morning, yet she smiled as she stepped onto the porch.

"Morning, ma'am."

All four men of her escort sent her the same greeting. Chenoa smiled into each of their eyes before she considered Kiril. The dark-eyed young man held the most rank of her escort and assumed the leadership position.

His frame was tall and broad. He was already coated in thick muscle but needed a few more years before command would sit squarely onto his shoulders.

"The morning is always the freshest after the rain comes."

Kiril aimed his serious eyes at her and granted her a rather rare smile. "Yes, ma'am, it is."

"I'd like to walk if it is well with you." Chenoa knew she didn't have to ask for Kiril's permission but her grandmother said men were prideful creatures. A wise woman learned to avoid stepping on their egos when she could. Asking Kiril his opinion from time to time cost her nothing. Kiril's eyes gleamed with approval before he spread an open palm out toward the desert morning.

Chenoa stepped away from the house and smiled. She would save her strength for Lee.

Yet as with any important matter it was the approach that was most important. Chenoa lifted her face and sighed. The truth was, she was bored. Never had she been so lazy in all her years. Being such a burden was a shame. Chenoa did not understand why Lee allowed it to be so.

There were no lazy men under his command. Besides, having something to do would keep her thoughts from worrying about things best left alone.

"Ah, Nacoma, where is your mischief when I need it most?" Chenoa muttered her words in a low voice, which the morning wind snatched away. The glow of the fence came into sight as she climbed a rise. Chenoa could almost hear her friend's laughter. The truth was they were not so far apart.

But the glowing blue fence might as well have been a thousand miles of burning sand.

* * * * *

Zeik felt sweat pop out on his head. More fluid collected and then ran in drops down his brow.

Oh God! How he loved the idea of money!

The bitch in front of him had plenty. She tossed a bundle of notes onto the desk then clicked her neatly manicured fingernails together as she waited.

Sweet bitch. Bet she always got her way too. Her clothes were the best. So now she was shopping for what she couldn't find in her lily clean world. Zeik intended to make certain she paid for it.

"Maybe I don't want the money." She looked down her nose at him. Zeik sneered at her before letting his eyes linger over her tits. "You need to treat a man just right if you want him to bring you presents."

Brenda felt her throat constrict as the toad laughed. He licked his lips as he stared at her breasts. But she deserved it. In the last five years she'd managed to toss every good thing in her life right into the toilet.

She owed Xan. Even if it meant dealing with this human garbage. Forcing the lump down her throat, Brenda ran her eyes over him. She toyed with a single button on her suit top as she decided how to get out of giving him sex today. He might still get it but she wasn't slow enough to not outwit him at least a few times.

Besides, what was one more anyway? She'd always walked down this road looking for her own rewards. At least this time there was a good reason behind her black market shopping trip.

Flicking the button open, Brenda traced the swell of her breasts with a long fingernail. Zeik licked his lips again and leaned across his desk. "Well, I might be willing to reward you..." She fingered a second button while leaning forward. "Once I get what I want."

The button stayed closed. Zeik frowned. "Don't stop. A man needs encouragement."

"So do I." Brenda looked down her nose at him again. The black market was always a game of will. But it always came down to money and sex. Oh yes, the scum that ran the underground always wanted their screwing included for free. It shouldn't bother her. She certainly hadn't been a virgin when she'd met Xan. Sex didn't mean anything. Well unless it was with Xan, then it became so much more.

She was so stupid.

"All right." Zeik scooped up the money and stuffed it into his shirt. His eyes traced her breasts again before he ducked out the door. Brenda didn't relax because she wasn't finished yet.

"That was real smooth." Brenda turned to face the man she'd hired to find Zeik. Just another example of a man who would sell anything to anyone and get his sex for free. His yellow teeth appeared as he smiled at her. One clumsy hand groped for her breast as he backed her into the now empty desk.

Brenda turned her head because a man like this enjoyed rape more than sex. But that didn't mean she didn't know how to deal with him. Curling her hand around his genitals, Brenda squeezed them just enough to promise him pain the next time. A snicker escaped his mouth as the pig drooled on her exposed cleavage.

"When I get my bitch, you'll get yours."

He stopped drooling as rage made his nostrils flare. His tongue took a swipe over his lips as he considered the rewards of waiting 'til Brenda was more willing. He raised a huge paw and struck her across the face with it. The blow flung her across the desk and he snickered louder as she scrambled to her feet again.

"I love a bitch that plays rough. Even an ice-cold one like you."

* * * * *

"Sir? We've got a problem."

Lee swung around in his chair because Xan didn't call something a problem unless it was on the verge of becoming a catastrophe. His lieutenant was clutching his helmet under his arm as he shook his head free of sand. The desert wind blew the tiny grains up into the enforcer helmets and made them itch like sin.

Xan thumped the helmet on its top to dislodge as much sand as possible. "You have to see this to believe it."

Grabbing his own helmet Lee headed for the door and the transport. It took them exactly five minutes to reach the gate. Lee pulled his helmet off because this threat wasn't covered by the codebook. His gate was pulsing as it was hit by objects being thrown at it.

From the inside.

"They started this morning at sunrise. We've got half a dozen messages from someone in there demanding we open the gate."

Lee considered the pulsing before he took a determined stride toward the operations center to look at the messages. Every last one was in his own language. These weren't primitives.

But they were Indians. The law was abundantly clear as to the fact that the Indians had to stay on the reservation. Lee ground his teeth together as he considered the fact that not a single Indian on that reservation knew about that law.

But if they found out, it might mean full-scale revolt. Maybe Lee didn't personally agree with locking them up but the human race had to survive. That much he agreed with.

But he'd still try to reason with them.

"Get a squad out there and prepare to open the gate."

Lee didn't wait for Xan's response. Instead he moved toward his gate and took up a stance ten feet from its glowing surface. The barricade shimmered before it dropped to revel some fifty Indians. Striding forward, Lee placed himself inside the gate itself. Exactly in the middle.

Young and old, they were all simply waiting. Several young women were closest to the gate, their clothing marked with sweat from their efforts to get the attention of the enforcers. They dropped their rocks the second the gate dissipated.

Lee surveyed the Indians with curious eyes. There had never been any contact between the enforcers and the inhabitants of the reservation. Now, the Indian council did communicate with the central command but as far as Lee knew the Indians were rather content to forget about the rest of the planet.

An elderly woman stood up from her seat on a large boulder. The rest of the group seemed to follow her with their eyes. She commanded attention with her long gray hair. Her face was etched with decades of wisdom, but her eyes were as sharp as a blade.

"We wish to see our daughter." She held her palm out to keep Lee silent as she searched the area behind him before speaking again. "Five daughters are missing this season. Chula saw one of the Peoples' children at this gate three days past. The families have come to see whose daughter still walks on the Mother Earth."

Her people stood behind her. Five different families seemed to have sent their members to the gate for their kin. He'd already realized that Chenoa had a life within the boundaries of the reservation. Looking at the hopeful eyes of each family group, he suddenly understood how much his own life lacked such a tight bond of blood.

"The one seen is named Chenoa." The smallest group present lifted their eyes in response. Lee watched the rest tighten their faces. When a victim was vaporized there wasn't any way to inform her family. Seeing the hope die on these faces tightened Lee's determination to find his pirate den.

The two members of Chenoa's family moved forward and the elder woman stopped them with her hand. An unspoken warning seemed to pass between the two old women. The younger one looked between her elders with a growing look of frustration.

"We must go to her." The woman who must have been Chenoa's grandmother shook her head at her companion. Deep sadness crossed the old Indian's face before she turned and walked away from the gate. The younger woman wasn't following. She stepped forward to be stopped by the second elder of the tribe.

"You will stop, Nacoma. You cannot cross onto the poisoned path of the modern man's world." Lee drew a sharp breath and the elder lifted her age-marked face toward him.

"Yes, I know the law." Her old voice was strangely calm as she spoke. "We helped to create it to protect our people. Yet it is not something to place upon the shoulders of the young. The burden would make them believe they are prisoners."

Nacoma's eyes grew large and round as she was firmly ordered to return to her spot next to Chenoa's grandmother. Both elders held resolved faces toward the young woman's frantically pleading eyes.

The old elder barked a single word at the young woman and she immediately set her face into a tight mask. The elder laid a soft hand onto the distended stomach of the girl as she issued low words that didn't reach Lee's ears.

He didn't need to hear them. The girl's unborn child was too precious to risk. He could never let her cross the gate.

Chenoa's own people wouldn't take her back. Relief crossed his mind in a rush too large to ignore. But anger came right on its heels. Being the one to bring that news to Chenoa was a task that twisted his gut.

But Lee still wasn't sorry. A lot of things were spinning through his skull. Sorrow wasn't one of them. Chenoa was staying in his world. That pleased the hell out of him, except for the rather large fact that it was going to break her heart into tiny fragments.

Nacoma lifted her head but her tight mask cracked as her eyes caught something beyond Lee. A sharp jerk of his head told Lee that Chenoa was taking her morning walk along the dunes. The housing compound was just too damn close to the gate.

Knowing her cousin was on Lee's side of the gate was one thing. Nacoma wasn't able to hold her emotions at bay when faced with the reality of Chenoa's presence right in front of her. The pregnant girl surged forward while her grandmother tried in vain to hold onto her.

Lee knew a hundred different ways to stop deviants. Being forced to handle a pregnant woman scared the hell out of him. He wasn't sure how to touch her without causing the precious unborn baby harm. He caught her forearms and held her out from his body. He couldn't step past the gate himself without risking contaminating the reservation. It was possible he, himself, carried whatever virus caused the sterility plague.

The Indian elder gave a sharp command that snapped her people to attention. The younger women pulled their pregnant sister from his grip and dragged her away from the gate.

The amazing thing was, it was completely silent. Lee could feel the weight of Nacoma's eyes as she was pulled through the sand with her feet plowing deep furrows in it.

And he knew all too well that Chenoa could move silently too. A sharp turn and he captured her wrist as she tried to pass him.

Lee stopped her in her steps. Chenoa raised startled eyes to him. "I am not breaking my word, Commander. Yet I would hug my grandmother. I will return—this I promised you."

The grip on her wrist tightened even more. The way he held her arm made the bones bow out straight. Any move on her part made the hold painful.

"I can't allow that." His hips twisted just slightly as Lee used his body as more of barrier to keep her from stepping forward any further. "I'm sorry."

And he was.

Chenoa gasped in horror as she read the regret on his face. His golden eyes were somber with grief, yet deadly firm with intent. Her eyes flew toward her grandmother. The only member of her family raised her hands in the ancient sign of farewell. Every member of the tribe mirrored it, except for Nacoma.

It simply couldn't be. Chenoa couldn't absorb the shock of it. Her feet stepped forward as her mind simply became numb. Lee lifted her from the sand, capturing her body as she desperately looked at her family for understanding.

The harsh glare of the fence stung her eyes instead. Tears pricked her eyes as she violently pushed away from Lee's strength. Everything pressed in on her. There were endless bodies of men all there to separate her from her family.

Chenoa shook her head in denial as her feet shuffled away from the glowing reminder of her exile. She couldn't look at the fence without knowing her grandmother stood behind it. She couldn't look at Lee without seeing the man who had lifted her away from her home.

But the ancient sign language was the most powerful blow. It stunned her with its intensity. Sign language was the only true tribal language that was universal to each and every tribe that now lived together on the reservation.

Those signs were used on only the most sacred of events. Birth, coming of age, marriage and lastly death. The fence meant nothing compared to the final parting sign from her people.

Chenoa could not return.

Hurt became a living thing inside her chest that beat its wings inside her. It grew so large that the very breath inside her lungs was forced out, leaving Chenoa with burning lungs that she couldn't seem to fill.

A childhood filled with obedience to the elders slammed into her head. The memories doubled the pain as she felt the walls collapsing onto her. Chenoa was helpless against the wave of hopelessness that swept her up into its grasp.

Lee stood silently in front of his gate, his golden eyes full of remorse yet his body firmly planted in front of her. His men surrounded them both with their weapons held in tight hands. She was snared in their trap as securely as any rabbit.

Chenoa turned and ran.

Pulling her feet out of the sand, she pushed herself away from her captors. The endless miles of sand were so very welcoming. Distance was relieving. She looked at the desert sand and found it the only familiar friend left to her.

"Kiril." The junior officer halted immediately and turned to his commanding officer.

Lee watched the pure symphony of Chenoa's strength. Her legs dug into the desert sand with strong movements that carried her over the dunes with amazing speed. "Let her work it out."

Chenoa disappeared over a dune. Lee shook his head again. He couldn't give her that much space. There was still a band of pirates out there. Chenoa didn't understand that she was running right into their claws.

"Take a transport and keep her in sight."

"Yes, sir."

Kiril turned on a sharp heel. Lee felt his gut twist even tighter as the man went to obey his command. Chenoa would hate the very sight of the junior enforcer officer. Lee knew it and tightened his resolve.

She would learn to live with the enforcers. Lee intended to make certain of it. The reason was plain. Chenoa belonged to him. Maybe he was the primitive one. But he wasn't letting her go.

She would come in when she ran out of strength. There simply wasn't any other place for her to go.

His face tightened into a deeper frown because it pleased the hell out of him to know she would come back to him.

* * * * *

She shouldn't feel so empty. Exhaustion brought Chenoa to her knees. The sand rose up in a thin cloud as she simply dropped her body to the desert floor. The tiny grains floated back down to the earth.

Her breaths came in shallow pants. The sun was a distant memory now as well. Just the edges of the horizon were streaked with ruby tongues of fire. But the night was slowly eating away at each beam of light, swallowing the life-giving warmth until nothing but darkness remained.

Now she knew why no one ever returned from outside the fence. Like a child her tribe had sheltered her. Having her innocence ripped away was too painful. Chenoa didn't have any defense against the flood of emotion.

She was drowning in hopelessness. Rejection sat laughing in her face as she was tossed about in the chilling current. Desolation wrapped its suffocating folds around her heart as she was dragged toward the depths of depression.

Nothing sat there. Absolutely nothing. The emotions swirled around her heart and fled, leaving Chenoa empty. A hollow shell that found each breath a chore to draw into her lungs.

"It's time to come in, Chenoa."

Exhaustion fled in a second as Lee's voice filled her ears. Chenoa jumped to her feet as anger burned along her nerves. Her body was so weak! Maybe if she'd never touched this man, her tribe would have welcomed her home.

"Don't." Solid authority delivered that single word. The commander's voice sounded like the snap of a whip. Chenoa felt her temper explode as he ordered her about again.

"I will not be obedient! To anyone!"

"Neither of us can change this, Chenoa. It's done."

"Yet you will enforce it!" She spat her words out like an accusation. For the very first time Lee witnessed panic flashing from her dark eyes. Despair was carved into her face as she stumbled away from him like some wounded animal.

Dehydration left her eyes sitting in shallow sockets. Lee frankly didn't know how she was keeping on her feet. Extending his hand, Lee held a small canteen of water toward her.

"Drink, Chenoa." He softened his voice. She tossed her head and refused him with her eyes. Lee took a solid step toward her with the water held up for her eyes. "We can do this the easy way or the hard way. But you will drink the water."

The truth of his words slapped her straight across her face. Chenoa looked at his huge body and cursed the unfairness of his physical superiority. She took the water because she just couldn't bear to have him touch her.

His piercing eyes watched her tip the water into her mouth. Chenoa wrinkled her nose because the water was stale. Everything in his world stank of death. She would wither and die outside the Peoples' land.

The water hit her stomach and the muscle cramped immediately as it leapt toward the much needed moisture. A groan escaped her lips as Chenoa sank back to her knees. The cramps became tighter as her body closed tightly around the fluid. The nerves screamed at her for depriving her body of water.

Lee's body surrounded her a second later. He caught the water before it rolled onto the sand. One hand threaded through the tangled strands of her hair to capture her head in a solid grip. His arm clasped her to his chest as he tipped the canteen into her mouth again.

Water flooded her mouth and ran down her cheeks. "Swallow it." He was ruthless. He would bend her to his will.

Chenoa swallowed the water and choked as some of it hit her windpipe. Lee listened to her cough before he tipped another portion of the fluid down her throat. Setting the canteen aside he sent his fingers along her stomach and worked at the muscles to loosen them.

She groaned in relief this time. Lee pushed to his feet and plucked her off the sand. She squirmed against his hold but he clamped her tighter into his embrace. Leaning down, Lee dropped his words right into her ear. "Adjust to it, Chenoa. You are my woman now and I will not let you run to your desert to die." Lee squeezed her tightly as she struggled against his words. But Lee simply turned toward his transport. Shock did amazing things to the strongest of men. All things considered, Chenoa was owed her moment of panic.

Angling her body into the transport with him, Lee never released her. Instead he smoothed a large hand over her chilled arm.

Chenoa stiffened under the contact. She didn't want comfort. It wasn't right! How could her body accept comfort when everything she held dear was stolen away from her? Enjoying his touch had to be wrong. So very wrong.

Yet her body was weak. Her strength suddenly deserted her, bleeding away and leaving her against the solid body that held her. Chenoa caught his scent as her small breaths pulled it into her head.

She smothered a groan as her body pulsed in reaction to his. Everything her grandmother had ever taught her didn't keep her body from yearning for his.

Lee never let her out of his embrace. Instead he carried her into his quarters and laid her on his bed. Her eyes were simply wounded now. Full of pain, but thankfully panic had been left out there in the sand.

Chenoa watched Lee. Caught between guilt and yearning, she didn't know what else to do. No answer came to her mind so she watched him, absorbing with her eyes the strength that radiated from his body. He was a warrior. In spirit and flesh. His hawk's eyes pierced her own, refusing to let her reject him.

Now that she had surrendered her body, he was coming for her soul as well. Chenoa struggled against it. Lee peeled his uniform off, displaying his skin to her eyes. Every ridge of muscle latched onto her primitive instincts. Words meant nothing. Instead his body displayed the clear proof of his superior qualities as a mate.

Chenoa felt her body quiver with need. Deep inside her, her blood heated and pooled in her center. Lee stripped his pants away. His golden eyes watched her stare at the blatant proof of his arousal. The swollen staff of his sex made her shift as her body responded to it.

The chill left her body as Chenoa covered his body with her eyes. She drank in his maleness. Her body wanted life. The female inside her wanted his touch as the ultimate confirmation of survival.

Details of life seemed meaningless.

Her heart accelerated as he reached for her. Lifted against him, Chenoa let her legs tangle with his. He tugged the dress over her head leaving her as nude as he was. The slide of their bare skin was rich with sensation. More than pleasure registered inside her mind. Chenoa found herself lost in pure satisfaction.

She wanted him and she wanted him to take her. His hand gently kneaded her bottom as he pressed his staff into her belly. Her feet never touched the floor. Instead Lee held her above it in a need to control her. Bind her to his strength. Insist she comply. He growled softly as his eyes battled with her stubborn refusal to surrender her entire person to him. She clung to her thoughts.

He carried her into the shower. Chenoa gasped as the cold water hit her. Lee lowered her feet to the floor as his hands began to bathe her. She shuddered. There was such raw emotion flowing from his face.

"Close your eyes." The word came on the heels of another low growl. Chenoa wavered with indecision. The level of compliance he was demanding took more than physical trust. The strength of his expression held her more securely than the strong hands that smoothed over her hair and moved to cradle her face.

Her dark eyes fell closed and Lee smiled. It was a primal expression that would have frightened her with its intensity.

Moving his hands into her hair, Lee washed it free of dirt. Too many forces in the world seemed to be wedged between them. He wasn't in the mood to allow it tonight.

Lee reached for the shampoo and began to wash her hair. The plain truth was he wanted to touch her. Soothe her, maybe even comfort her. But there was also a burning desire to brand her. Make certain she never separated herself from him completely.

Chenoa felt even smaller with her eyes closed. Her lips actually lifted into a faint smile as she remembered the feeling from the first time she'd met Lee. She pulled a deep breath into her lungs and felt her body jump with arousal. Her breasts lifted against his chest. She rubbed her nipples into him, delighting as he gasped.

But he never stopped washing her. His hands stroked and rubbed at her as the water poured over them both. Yet Chenoa felt boldness rise inside her. She wasn't feeling submissive. Being in his embrace was simply right. She wanted her mate and would not be denied.

His hands felt amazing on her skin. Chenoa absorbed the contact. Running a single hand down his body she closed her fingers around the throbbing rod of his sex. Lifting her eyelids, Chenoa watched his eyes darken with pleasure as she stroked the weapon in her hand.

"Do you want me, Chenoa?"

Her dark eyes were almost liquid with heat. She stroked his rod with tight fingers and nodded. Rolling a nipple between his finger and thumb, Lee gently pinched it.

"Say it. Tell me what you want." Capturing her head Lee covered her mouth and boldly kissed her. It was pure invasion. His tongue swept inside and demanded a response.

Chenoa kissed him back as she held the throbbing length of him in her hand. He thrust his tongue in time with that throbbing and her sex answered with an intense pulsing of its own. His kiss was arrogant with demand, forceful with need, as he tasted every inch of her flesh.

Punching the water off, Lee pulled her out of the shower. Ripping a towel off a rack Lee applied it to her long dark hair. Chenoa almost purred as his hands rubbed her head and neck. It was so very pleasurable. His aroused staff was pressed into her bottom even as he worked on her hair.

The folds of her sex began to quiver as she considered just how he would feel inside her passage again. Heat rose in her face as she recalled exactly how he'd brought her to her pleasure the last time they'd mated. If his mouth brought such pleasure to her sex, would hers do the same to his rod?

Turning within his embrace, Chenoa slowly dropped to her knees. His body was so very strong. She trailed her palms over each ridge of muscle as she went down his length. Wrapping her fingers around his rod, she pressed a tiny kiss onto the top of it. His breath made a harsh sound and she let her tongue lick his flesh next.

Lee curled his hand into her hair, unable to do anything but groan. It took every ounce of self-discipline he had to not come when she wrapped her lips around his staff. Her tongue flicked over him in teasing motions that kept his breathing harsh.

He pulled her head away, making Chenoa frown. She looked up into his face as he gently tugged her to her feet. "You did not like this?"

A hair's breadth from climax, Lee lifted her from her knees. "Your innocence amazes me. I loved it." Carrying her into his bedroom, he lowered her to his bed Lee clenched his teeth and controlled the urge to drop onto her. The animal inside him was full of her scent, hard and ready to stake his claim between her thighs. There was nothing gentle about it. He wanted to take her, hard, fast, and pump his seed deep inside her body.

"Then why did you stop me?" Chenoa gasped as he thrust into her body. He curled his lips back to show her clenched teeth. The hard thrust of his sex captured her attention as she found his actions soothing to her overheated flesh.

Chenoa flung her head back as she lifted her hips to his rhythm. Life's details fled as her body became a link in the chain of flesh. His and hers, they were simply one body.

Pleasure shattered her and Chenoa went willingly into its bliss. She didn't want to think. She wanted to feel only what her body felt, drown in the pure current of sensation.

Lee watched her body sink into slumber. Chenoa had the right idea but there wasn't any way he was going to be able to turn his mind off. Somehow, he'd actually believed he might be able to get her home.

That was a dead mission now. Suspecting her people might reject her was one thing. Now, he didn't have any choice but to face dealing with her future. Gently stroking her face, Lee frowned.

Chenoa's skin was rough and hot. He should have dragged her inside long before sunset. Adjusting her body, Lee enjoyed her weight against him. He turned his mind to the puzzle in front of him.

He wasn't planning on crying defeat...ever. Chenoa would adjust to his world and to him. He would make certain of that.

Chapter Eight

Chenoa slept past sunrise again. Raising her head took too much effort. Her mouth was as dry as the sand. Bringing order to her hair stung her eyes with tears. The desert was very unforgiving to those foolish enough to forget its dangers.

If Lee had not come for her she would have died.

Forcing her feet under her, Chenoa walked to the front door. Her muscles were tense and hard from lack of water. She must move her legs or the pain would last twice as long. Chenoa raised her chin and gritted her teeth. Foolishness was always paid for. The sooner she began, the sooner it would be over.

"Good morning."

Chenoa felt her cheeks color with embarrassment. How could she have forgotten her escort? She raised her chin but looked into Xan's light-colored eyes instead of Kiril's serious, dark ones.

Those light-colored eyes moved over her face with precise movements. He stepped closer as he reached for her hand but suddenly stopped. "Lee warned me to ask you before I touched you." He said it lightly with a smile tugging the corners of his lips up. His eyes sparkled with amusement.

"Why do you want to touch me?"

"I'm the Medical Officer. It looks like you've got a rather severe burn on those hands."

Chenoa simply nodded her head. It appeared she was going to have more witnesses to her rash behavior. She looked at her hands and grimaced as she saw tiny blisters sprinkled across the backs of both of them.

Xan made a deep sound in his throat and indicated a chair on the porch for her to sit in. Chenoa dropped into it like a child waiting for her chastisement to begin. His large hands were light as he searched her body for injury.

"Good thing your hair is so thick or your head would be covered with blisters too." Pulling his medical kit onto his lap, Xan began to rub a lotion into her hands. "This will keep it from scarring."

He reached for her face and she jumped in surprise. He raised an eyebrow before moving toward her again. His hands were firm as he applied more of the lotion to her forehead. Chenoa found most of her pain lifting away within seconds.

"Now for the hard part." Chenoa looked at the lieutenant with curious eyes. Pulling another item from his bag he raised the slim box toward her eyes.

"Hold still and don't blink." The thing hummed slightly before he turned it toward his face and studied it.

"Well, at least you didn't do any damage to your eyes." Those light eyes of his turned hard as he aimed a firm look at her. "You will stay out of the sun until the blisters are gone."

"I will simply cover them."

"Don't be stubborn."

Chenoa lifted her chin. "I was not raised to be lazy. To sit about is to be a burden."

Xan considered her thoughtfully. "All right, but you are to stay off the dunes today. In bed would be even better." She pressed her lips together and Xan stood up. "Drink lots of water then." Xan dug something else out of his medical kit. "I want to give you an infusion of Gyseratel. It will aid your immune system."

Chenoa nodded her approval and he reached for her wrist. Turning her arm over he pressed the slim rod in his hand to her skin. Pressure was the only sensation and then he replaced the device in its kit. He produced a small bottle of pills, which he offered to her. Chenoa curled her fingers around the bottle.

"That's more Gyseratel. Take one at each meal."

"Thank you."

Xan's eyes considered her again. He lifted his mouth into that grin but this time it didn't reach his eyes. "Hungry?"

"Well...no." In fact, the very idea of food made her gag. Chenoa slapped a hand over her mouth as she fought the urge to retch. Horror flooded her as she realized how little strength she had to fight her body's reactions. She wasn't even strong enough to overcome the idea of food. Swallowing her nausea took a great deal of her remaining strength. A fine tremor was left behind as her body became chilled.

"Chenoa?"

"Yes, Lieutenant?" Her voice shook as well and her face turned red with embarrassment.

"Would you like to walk or be carried back to your bed?"

Humiliation might be crowing with victory, yet Chenoa would fight it every step of the way. "I *will* walk!"

* * * * *

"Thanks, Xan, I owe you one." Lee considered his lieutenant as relief spread over his shoulders. Lee hadn't realized just how tense he was. Chenoa had that effect on him. A crooked smile crossed his face as Lee considered just how many ways his little Chenoa disrupted his life.

He wasn't complaining. Just trying to keep up.

"Technically, it's my job." Xan dropped into his terminal's chair behind Lee. The outpost was pitifully small in order to conserve resources. Like the amount of electricity that it took to keep the temperature civil inside the station, private offices were a luxury Lee didn't indulge in.

"But you're welcome anyway."

Lee turned back to Russell's latest communication. The man wanted Chenoa delivered to the witness protection center. The fact that the man had sent his request in electronic form was rather telling. It was still a request but that wouldn't be lasting too much longer. This way Russell had a record and he didn't have to face Lee while doing it.

Flipping to another message, Lee dismissed Russell. The man might be a good manager but Lee was sitting on the reservation outpost because he was the commander with field experience.

In short, Russell might demand all he wanted but Lee was the man who could get the job done. Russell knew that. He wouldn't shake Lee's tree too hard.

A shadow crossed the doorway and stayed. Lee turned his head to find Brenda standing in the doorframe. The woman was pitifully thin. Maybe Chenoa was giving him a new slant on women because his lieutenant's estranged spouse looked like a sack of bones to him.

Brenda looked at Xan like a lost mirage. Lee's junior officer wasn't in much better shape. The two were staring at each other like wounded animals.

"I found them. But they want something from you before they will bring me the merchandise." She held a small silver disk out toward Xan. It was a micro image recorder that she'd used to record her meeting with Zeik. The toad had looked straight into it while trying to look down her blouse. It matched the buttons on her suit perfectly.

"How did you get out here, Brenda?"

Lee wanted to know the answer to Xan's question too. The woman in the doorway simply shrugged her thin shoulders. She aimed her blue eyes at Lee and grinned slightly.

"Your friend is rather resourceful and you told me not to use the communications terminal." She held her palms up into the air with another shoulder shrug. "I'm here."

Lee was impressed. Xan sat up straight as he considered the lengths his ex-wife had gone to. The effort wasn't lost on either of them.

"I told the guys on the transport we were giving it another try. Sorry, I couldn't think of a better reason to be on my way here."

Lee raised an eyebrow as he considered just exactly how his friend had gotten orders that allowed Brenda onto the transport. That sort of ability would make any commander nervous, but in this case Lee was also impressed. He ran a tight outpost.

But Javier Trey was a recluse who prompted more questions than the man ever answered. Lee considered it a major part of the man's charm. Lee felt a low rumble of laughter shake his chest. Javier would likely take any comment concerning charm as an invitation to fight. The man enjoyed being considered uncivilized. But he was also one of the richest men on the globe and an essential part of Lee's plan to outflank his pirates.

"Then I guess we'd better look a little bit happier to see each other." Xan stood up and pulled Brenda into a light embrace. He laid a tender kiss along her hairline before he froze and used a hand to push her short hair away from her face. "Who hit you?"

Brenda tossed her head to make her hair fall back into place along her face. Xan tightened his hold and refused to release her. Xan kept his voice low because the station was filled with fresh recruits. Any one of them might be prone to running his mouth.

"Who did that to your face, Brenda?" Xan pressed a hard kiss to her angry lips and pulled her closely into his body. "Remember you came here to see me, honey. Your story, so put your arms around me and stop wriggling."

Brenda draped her arms around Xan's neck. God she loved the feel of the man. She was caught between the need to melt against him or cry. She felt a deep quiver inside her belly in response to him. It had always been like that. From the first moment she'd seen him all she wanted was Xan.

Crossing the law had been her mistake. Xan could forgive her desperation to have his child but he would never forgive her illegal activity. Xan was an enforcer.

Smoothing a light kiss of her own on his chin, Brenda whispered into his ear. "The people you want to see aren't exactly nice. Let it go, it's only a bruise." Brenda slid out of Xan's embrace and moved across the office.

"Brenda, I didn't tell you to do anything dangerous."

"It would have been dangerous for me to give the scumbag the sex he wanted. Instead he slapped me for being a frigid bitch. I consider the bruise the better end of the deal."

Xan's face became a mask of fury. Lee wasn't far behind. Brenda narrowed her eyes at them both. "Excuse me. Did either of you think this was going to be a tea party? These people vaporize their captives and you are surprised over a slap or two?" Brenda crossed her hands over her chest. "Besides, I got the job done. Something tells me you two have collected a few bruises along the way in your jobs. So let's drop the whole protective attitude. I found your supplier."

"How sure are you of that?" Lee wasn't dropping the issue but he wasn't going to lose the information Brenda had either.

"He says he's got an Indian already off the reservation and a man sitting out in the sand watching her. Promised me a timely delivery when I come through with his demands." Brenda tossed a small picture onto Lee's desk. The blurred image was Chenoa twirling around in the rain.

Brenda was grateful she was standing across the room. Both men became images of fury, so tightly controlled inside their huge bodies.

Lee felt a surge of power cross his mind. *Damn.* He was right. Russell could choke on his politically correct decisions. Now that both sides of the chain were in sight all Lee had to do was tie them into a knot that wouldn't allow even one pirate to slip through.

"What do they want?"

"The security codes to the camera on the housing compound."

Eyeing the picture of Chenoa again Lee grinned. It must be driving them crazy to watch their prey and never be able to scoop her up. His lips set back into a firm line though as he considered Chenoa being hunted. The harsh reality of her value hit Lee right between the eyes. Russell, pirates...everyone seemed to be fighting over her like a scrap of meat.

Lee knew how to deal with deviants but he still didn't have a clue how to deal with the rest of the planet. Exactly how did he go about educating the world? Chenoa was a person but they saw her as a commodity. It was an ignorance he'd suffered from himself.

"The transport is full, no room for passengers on the return trip." Lee stood up and tossed a hard look at Xan. His lieutenant considered him from his chair before he gave a hard nod.

Xan aimed his eyes at his wife. Brenda's eyes widened in shock before she opened her mouth to argue. Lee simply left the room. Brenda kept her voice low but the tone was unmistakably outraged.

Brenda was a citizen, therefore entitled to her freedom. But Lee commanded the outpost and didn't have to make it easy for her to get back to the city. Considering the bruises along her face, Lee decided there wasn't going to be any room on his transports 'til he and Xan finished their mission.

* * * * *

Chenoa lifted her head and squinted at the setting sun. A low growl of frustration escaped her throat as she swung her legs off the bed.

Yet another wasted day. She would die of shame if the pattern continued. There had to be something for her to do on the compound. Taking care of two chickens wasn't nearly enough.

Suddenly she stopped and sniffed at the air. Something stank in the room. Turning about Chenoa decided the smell was somewhat familiar. Only she couldn't remember just where she had smelled the odor before. But she did not like it.

With complete horror she discovered that the stench was coming from her own skin. Lifting her arm she sniffed at her skin and wrinkled her nose. Never had she ever smelled so foul!

Turning sharply about she headed for the shower. Her face turned crimson as she recalled rather vividly her last shower.

Her stomach growled but the odor was too strong to ignore. Chenoa applied the soap to her skin with determination. Turning the water to a hotter temperature she scrubbed her body from head to toe. The hot water stung her sunburn but Chenoa refused to stink.

A faint scent lingered despite her best efforts. Chenoa stepped into the evening breeze as she tried to leave the smell behind. The chickens were cleaning their nests so she went to collect their eggs.

Pulling two eggs from the nest, Chenoa frowned. Two eggs. Her grandmother's flock would produce twenty eggs each day. Yet these two eggs were her only protein. Less than a mile separated her from the market where food was everywhere you looked.

Here Chenoa was grateful for her two eggs.

She shook her head almost violently. She must not cry. It was over. Nothing would change. What was she to do? Search for a way back to her people? That would do her no good.

Again it came back to the fence. As the sun set, the blue glow lit up the horizon. Chenoa raised her eyes toward it. Protection or prison? It was the same thing to her now.

Two enforcers drifted into her line of sight and she felt those tears pricking her eyelids. Lee told her nothing. He'd known and treated her exactly like a child. She could not dismiss it.

The man didn't think she could shoulder the weight of such things. She was a woman grown enough for him to take her to his bed, yet still he left her innocent of the truth that surrounded her.

Chenoa angrily wiped her eyes. She would not cry! She refused to act like a child, even if Lee treated her like one. Resentment rose inside her. Chenoa felt herself despising everyone who sheltered her. Now that she was left alone, their protection was becoming her most difficult obstacle to scale.

Her own ignorance was tangling her feet so that she couldn't even walk. Instead she was crawling on her hands and fighting for even an inch of room. The enforcers kept walking. Chenoa considered them with knowing eyes.

Tilting her head she looked behind her. Lee always appeared silently just like the hawk she saw in his eyes. He stood watching her. The silent stance was so very powerful. The warrior inside him was only lightly covered by the trappings of society.

This man was a predator. The animal stared out of him through his golden raptor eyes. Even blind, Chenoa had sensed it. Her body leapt again as he watched her. She felt her limbs quiver in response.

Lifting her chin, Chenoa pressed her lips into a firm line. It seemed unfair to respond to him so quickly. She didn't seem to even have a say over her flesh. Her skin began to tingle as heat ran in streams through her body. She wanted to ignore him, refuse to melt into desire at his very presence.

A low chuckle was her response. Only it came from another man who stood to her right. Chenoa considered him. Another warrior. Chenoa had no doubt about that fact. The man wore his strength on his powerful frame but his eyes were burning with a flame as wild as a firestorm.

He nodded his head as one single corner of his mouth twitched up in greeting. His dark eyes simply remained a roaring blaze of flame. Chenoa decided he and Lee were good company for each other. Both were warriors who fed off their battles. Each conflict made them stronger. It was something she might be able to notice yet never share. She was separated from the depths of the emotion by her gender.

Chenoa simply raised her chin. Male and female were different. It was not something to lament. But it was something to remember.

"There's nothing quite like fresh eggs."

Chenoa gently tightened her grasp on her eggs and waited to see what this man wanted. Lee seemed content to watch them.

"But I prefer duck eggs."

Chenoa believed him. A duck egg was much stronger in flavor than a chicken's. "These eggs are precious because they are fresh."

"Ahhh."

Lee suddenly grinned. It was a wide expression that showed his teeth. "Chenoa doesn't think very much of the enforcers' provisions."

"I agree with her." The man walked closer. Chenoa stood firmly in her spot because he was testing her. The flames in his eyes had become brighter. He loomed over her a second before a full smile covered his face. Lee appeared between them and caught the eggs as he pulled her away from his friend, raising one of her hands to his face. Lee inspected the blisters. His eyes aimed harsh reprimand at her before he let her pull away.

"This is Javier. He's a friend of mine. Sometimes." The man name Javier laughed. He tilted his head toward Lee and smiled most unpleasantly.

"Careful, Lee. She might be worth losing your friendship." Javier touched her cheek lightly. Chenoa immediately slapped his hand away. Yet she wasn't angry with the man. His touch was only annoying, not hot like Lee's.

"You are like boys in the school yard, pulling the braids of all the girls."

Chenoa shook her head as both men laughed. It was a deep rumble of male amusement. She tossed her braids over her shoulders and went toward the house. This was not a place for a female. Indeed she just might swat their ears like naughty boys if she remained.

Javier sobered the second she left. His eyes watched the sway of her hips too keenly for Lee's comfort. Javier didn't miss the tight mask that covered Lee's face in response.

"Relax, Lee. I don't poach."

"Fine. Get your eyes off my woman."

Javier didn't laugh. Instead the man gave Lee a deep considering look. Appreciation for Chenoa was written in his friend's eyes in the most basic of manners. The flame brightened as it bordered on lust. Lee sent the man a clear warning with his own eyes.

"Well, then." Javier sent another look at Chenoa. "Be a pal and let me know if you become stupid enough to let her go. I'd like the chance to join the fray for her."

"Over my dead body."

"Me claiming her? Or the frenzied clamoring of every politically connected man on the globe?" Javier took another look at Chenoa before sliding his hard look back at Lee. "They'll fight over her like a pack of wild dogs."

It was a good question. Lee considered Chenoa's hips again as arousal snaked through his body along a familiar path. Javier's eyes were hot as he waited for an answer. Lee didn't think there was another man on the planet Javier would have asked permission from.

"Chenoa is mine."

Possessiveness was new. Lee considered the emotion and growled. It was a low sound of deep fury. He'd always prided himself on his detachment. Javier had truly enjoyed rubbing salt into Lee tonight.

Walking through the dark house, Lee found he didn't care. After all, Chenoa was sleeping in his bed tonight so Javier could enjoy himself as he saw fit. Just so long as it wasn't anywhere near Chenoa.

Lee came to an abrupt stop in the doorway to his room. The bed was empty. Turning around he moved through the darkness like a shadow. Chenoa was curled up on her bed against the wall tonight. The stark change didn't escape his notice.

The moonlight spilled over the bed but she was pressed to the wall. Hidden in the shadow as she tried to escape life's harsh reality. Lee considered her attempt to push him away and turned back toward his room.

It took exactly five seconds to yank his uniform off. Lee walked back toward Chenoa and simply scooped her sleeping body off the bed. He clamped her against his chest as she erupted into a bundle of frantic movement.

"Put me down." He squeezed her instead. Chenoa strained against him. "I want to sleep in my own bed."

Lee dropped her onto his bed instead. She rolled free of her blanket and tried to jump off the bed. The moonlight hit his body and Chenoa froze. He was truly magnificent. His body was so foreign in her world yet she seemed to know it was made to fit with her own. None of it made any sense to her emotions.

"This is your bed." Lee rolled onto the bed and pulled her body along with his. He pressed her onto her back as he propped himself up on an elbow next to her. One powerful leg tangled with both of hers and kept her pinned to the sheets. He nudged her thighs apart with his knee as she tried to keep her distance.

Chenoa felt her tears return. She was as helpless as the tiny drops squeezed out of her eyes. She pushed against Lee's chest but he simply rubbed his huge hands over her in comfort. She couldn't seem to escape. His strength seeped through her body and right into her soul.

Lee pressed warm kisses along her hairline. Chenoa struggled against him because she wanted to go... Instead he held her to his body, his strength surrounding her.

"Let me be."

Lee pulled her closer even as she tried to untangle their limbs. He smoothed a hand over her cheek and felt the heat of her emotions. "You aren't alone. I won't let you run into your desert or across these quarters."

His hands settled along her face and lifted it to his eyes. His mouth captured hers in a kiss that demanded complete surrender. His tongue swept inside her mouth and boldly mastered her.

Surrendering her kiss to him made passion flare between their bodies. His rod thickened against her thigh as he thrust his tongue into her mouth in a pulsing rhythm. Chenoa felt her sex pulse with that very same rhythm. Her hips jerked with small movements that encouraged his staff as it swelled and hardened.

Lee never stopped kissing her. Instead he rolled over her body, settling into the cradle of her thighs. She opened toward his staff and he thrust into her body with the same rhythm as his tongue.

It wasn't sex. Instead it was a deep moment of intimacy. Lee thrust into her passage with deep strokes that made her hips jerk toward him. He growled into her mouth as she gasped and lifted her hips again.

"Our bed. This is our bed. Do you understand me, Chenoa?" Lee ground his hips against hers as his lips slashed across hers once again. Lifting his head, he aimed his eyes into her dark ones. "Say it, Chenoa. Our bed."

Lee stopped moving. His huge body pinned her beneath him as his staff twitched inside her passage. His hawk's eyes were relentless. His demand hung in the air while her body was balanced on the edge of sensation.

"It's our bed."

He thrust again as she gasped with pleasure. "Say, 'It's our bed, Lee'."

She hit him instead. Lee moved between her legs and groaned as his staff refused to stop at the wet entrance of her body.

Chenoa felt the walls of her passage stretching to allow him deeper. His hips were relentless as he thrust forward into her deepest center. She ripped her mouth from his as she felt him touch her womb. Sensation so sharp it was almost painful as it ripped through her belly. Chenoa heard her own voice hit the night but couldn't stop the sound. She could only endure the waves of pleasure as Lee ground his staff into her belly and spilled his seed into her.

Lee rolled off her and pulled her body along his. Wrapping a blanket around her, he smoothed her into perfect alignment with his body. Chenoa didn't have any tears left in her. She simply didn't understand. Maybe she never would. But she understood one thing very clearly.

"It's our bed, Lee."

A warm hand cupped her face and raised it. Chenoa felt his eyes inspecting her face. His hand moved over her head, warmly stroking her hair.

"If you forget that, Chenoa, I'll be happy to remind you."

* * * * *

"You should not be so disgraceful."

Nacoma didn't answer but her aunt wasn't expecting her to anyway. The elder shook a finger in Nacoma's face and continued.

"The Elders know best."

Her aunt gave a huff and left. Nacoma breathed a sigh of relief. Truly she had not known a week could last so long! It was endless. Everyone seemed to know what was best for her.

Forget Chenoa. Poor Chenoa. A terrible thing that has happened to Chenoa. But always it came back to simply...forget.

What kind of friend forgot the look of anguish in her best friend's eyes? Forget? Nacoma was certain it was written across her heart. If not there, her tears had certainly left the sorrow stained on her cheeks.

"Someone so pretty shouldn't be so sad."

Nacoma jumped and stared into a pair of serious eyes. She had foolishly been walking with no care as to where her feet took her. She immediately stepped away from the competitor. In her foolishness she all but walked into the man.

"You should not be here." Nacoma knew she sounded harsh but she didn't care. She must hold her tongue with her elders but this competitor was no one to the people. His face tightened and she felt her cheeks flush with regret. Chenoa would have yanked one of her braids if her friend heard her behaving so poorly.

"I am sorry. I spoke harshly."

The competitor let his face return to its serious expression. Nacoma let her eyes wander over the man. He was very large. Yet he was wearing a large shirt that was buttoned to his neck. He'd rolled the cuffs up to let his wrists catch the breeze but that was all. The fact that he wasn't flaunting his bare skin made him quite unique. Every competitor she'd ever seen had been forward.

"Can I ask you a question?" His politeness further confused Nacoma. She nodded her head as she shifted and tried to understand why the man wasn't doing something vulgar to get her into his bed.

"Is that a baby?"

A smile burst across her face as Nacoma rubbed her belly. Her child was her only source of joy. This man's eyes looked at her belly like it was the most sacred of shrines. She would swear he was holding his breath waiting for her to answer his question.

"Yes, I will birth a child soon. Have you never seen a woman with her babe beneath her heart before?"

He shook his large head and used those dark serious eyes to caress her swollen belly. "You're so beautiful."

His voice was rough with emotion. Her baby gave a large kick and Nacoma smiled. She reached for the competitor's hand. He raised confused eyes but let her lay his hand over her belly. The hand went flying away a second later when her baby kicked it.

Nacoma let her silvery laugh escape her lips. "What is your name?" She liked this man. Chenoa had said that there must be nice modern men somewhere. It was almost like having her friend with her to discover her words ringing true through this serious-eyed competitor.

"Kiril." He recovered himself quickly and reached his hand back toward her. Nacoma laid it along her child's movements and watched his face light with amazement.

"Chenoa was right." The words slipped out of Nacoma's mouth as a whisper. Kiril raised sharp eyes to her as he frowned.

"Did you know Chenoa?" Kiril almost swore out loud a second later. The emotion of the moment had gone straight to his head. The Indian girl looked at him with a deep longing in her dark eyes. It softened his face. Besides, he doubted she was a pirate.

"Chenoa is my best friend. You have seen her?" Nacoma's eyes pleaded for just a little information. "She was outside when you came onto the Peoples' land?"

Kiril felt his lips lift into a grin. He did miss his little guard duty assignment. But he was itching for the chance to sink his teeth into a real enforcer matter. Hunting pirates fit that bill nicely.

But the afternoon was warm and lazy. For the moment Kiril could enjoy Chenoa's friend. An enforcer didn't get many chances to indulge his own desires.

* * * * *

Chenoa slept the day away again. Yet she truly didn't care so very much. A naughty little smile crossed her face as she once again noticed that Lee had left her feeling sore. Heading for the shower she considered that her grandmother would have approved of Lee.

Yes, Lee was a fine warrior.

A slight odor still clung to her skin. Chenoa washed herself, trying to be rid of it. She had suffered sunburns before, so it must have been in the medicine Xan had given her.

Drifting back into the bedroom she picked up the bottle of pills the man had left her.

Sniffing at them Chenoa wrinkled her nose. How did modern women endure the stench? She shoved them into a drawer. She had done well enough without them all her life and Chenoa decided she was not interested in stinking. Her body would heal as it always had, as nature intended.

The sun hung low in the sky. Chenoa stepped out to enjoy the evening. Lee would return soon. She found her face lifting into another smile as she considered welcoming him home. Her body felt refreshed now, healed from her rash day in the sun. She was fortunate she healed so quickly. Some people took over a week to recover from exposure.

Maybe Xan's medicine was to thank for that. Chenoa winkled her nose again. She was not so injured that she was willing to stink. The blisters would heal well enough without the foul smelling drugs.

"You must be Chenoa."

Chenoa gasped and turned immediately. The unexpected female voice was so welcome to her ears.

"Hello. I'm Brenda. There's no one around to introduce us so I just thought I'd do it myself."

Chenoa returned the hesitant smile Brenda offered her. The woman looked at the eggs Chenoa held with confusion. "What are those?"

Chenoa found it difficult not to laugh. What manner of life did these modern women lead that led to them not knowing something so common? Brenda was as thin as a rail. Chenoa smiled as she considered what the woman needed.

"These are eggs. I am going to cook them for supper. Come inside and we will share them."

"Thank you." Brenda muttered the words because she wasn't so sure she would be happy with the outcome of the invitation. She'd heard that the Indians were primitives. That didn't promise her any kind of tasty meal ahead. But Brenda followed Chenoa anyway. Xan seemed to be in full agreement with his commander about stranding her on the outpost. Sampling the Indian girl's cooking would be worth the effort just for some feminine company.

Chenoa scooped up the eggs from the day before and added them to her current two. It would make a small meal. New fruit had arrived as well.

Brenda sniffed at the air and then sniffed again. Her stomach let out a low rumble in response. She laughed. It had been a very long time since she'd been hungry. Actually it had just been a long time since she'd looked forward to anything.

"My grandmother taught me to cook eggs like this." Chenoa slid a plate in front of her guest and watched the woman inspect the meal with hesitant eyes. Chenoa lifted a forkful of the dish into her own mouth as Brenda watched. The woman copied Chenoa exactly. Her face lit up as she chewed the food.

"Now I see why people pay a fortune for fresh eggs. This is decadent." The flavor was so intense. Brenda closed her eyes to savor it. She didn't think her tongue had ever been so sensitive before.

"Eggs are expensive in your world?"

"Ummm… Yes." Brenda chewed her next mouthful slowly in order to make it last longer.

Chenoa reached for an orange and began to peel it. Brenda sniffed at the air again as the smell of the fruit drifted with that of the eggs. "My grandmother would be a rich woman then. She keeps too many chickens for just herself. I often give away the eggs so that they are not wasted."

"But chickens are so expensive to keep!"

Chenoa shook her head. "On the Peoples' land it is a simple thing. The most trouble is keeping the rooster out of the hen's yard. But like all males he is very persistent. There always seems to be a nest of chicks to confirm that."

"Well, I just might be willing to endure the cost after tasting how good these eggs are." Brenda reached into her pocket and pulled a small bottle out. She tipped it up and two pills were left in her hand. She offered the bottle to Chenoa.

"Do you need some Gyseratel? Especially with fresh food, you should take some. You wouldn't want your immune system to lower."

Chenoa winkled her nose. "Why do you take that? You are strong and healthy."

Brenda looked at the pills and back at Chenoa. "Well, it's just a good habit. You know, prevention. Especially with all this germ warfare in the world now. You can never be too careful."

"If one is lazy their body becomes weak. Taking that every day would make the body unable to be strong. Besides, it smells so foul."

Brenda lifted the pills to her nose and sniffed them. "You know, I've never noticed that they have a scent." She sniffed the pills again but shook her head. "Besides it's in almost everything—food, water, even candy."

Chenoa laughed. "That explains why your food stinks." Brenda dropped the pills back into the bottle and took the segments of orange Chenoa offered her. The woman closed her eyes in pure ecstasy when she tasted the fruit. Brenda chewed thoughtfully for a moment before she shoved the bottle back into her pants pocket.

"Well, I have to say this is the tastiest meal I've ever had so maybe you're right. Forget the Gyseratel and hand me some more of that orange thing."

* * * * *

"God damn it all! Javier Trey is out there? Keep him the hell away from my Indian!" Russell was shouting into the communications line. Lee found himself more than just annoyed. He was getting angrier by the second.

"Russell, if you want to replace me, fine."

"Hey, now don't get so hot, Lee. I need you out there." Russell backpedaled at full speed. "But I've got plans for that girl. Important plans. Keep Javier away from her. That's all I'm saying."

Lee ground his teeth together. Javier stood behind the console listening to Russell's every word with a self-satisfied smirk on his face. Russell ended the call seconds later. Lee felt his temper skyrocket as Javier threw his head back and laughed. "The fray has begun. Does Chenoa have any idea what asses inhabit this globe?"

"No, she doesn't." Lee stood up and moved toward his transport. "And it's going to stay that way. "

"I can't wait to see how you plan to keep that promise, buddy."

"Shut up."

Javier laughed instead. The man's shoulders shook as he filled the office with his amusement. Lee growled as the tension twisting in his gut became acute.

"Come on, buddy, you've had your fun. Why don't you introduce me and put in a good word for me?"

Lee's chair hit the deck as he surged out of it. No one was going to introduce Javier to his woman! Javier's face suddenly lost any trace of amusement. His body tensed as he faced off with Lee.

"Come on, Lee, you chose that uniform. Russell won't be the only man that expects you to turn her over. They won't even care that you broke her in for them."

Harsh, but true. Lee ground his teeth together as rage began to twist along his spine. Fury seemed to erupt from every cell in his body as he considered the blunt truth of Javier's words. The man was right. No one would even consider leaving Chenoa in his care, even if she asked to stay there. The need to chain her to him clawed up inside him as he tried to find the method of keeping her away from the greedy men lining up to take his place in her bed.

The solution was as primitive as his rage. A custom left behind as impulse became the normal mode of operation. Sex might be casual but marriage was still legally binding.

Lee raised an eyebrow. "Why don't you stick around for a bit and you can watch. I'll be back."

Pride shot straight through Lee the second he entered his bedroom. Chenoa was in *his* bed. Exactly where she belonged. Rage transformed into pride as he considered making certain she would always be sleeping in his bed. Moonlight bathed her body as her chest rose in deep movements. Lee pulled the frail scent of his female into his nose. Her eyelids lifted to show him the deep liquid pools of her eyes.

She rose up onto an elbow and gave him that innocent smile of hers. Lee held his hand out to her. "Come here, Chenoa."

His commanding tone didn't really bother her tonight. Chenoa had to be honest. It was simply part of Lee's strength. Here in their bedroom she could not deny how very attracted she was to his power. She found her body drawn to it, to him. Like she didn't want to be apart but endured it while life forced them to be practical and productive during the day.

Here in the dark, it was simply strength and need. Lee demanded and she craved him. His hand closed gently around hers as her feet found the floor. Lee pressed tiny kisses along her neck before pulling a deep breath into his chest.

"Do you trust me?" His arm bound her to his body with gentle strength. Being surrounded by his power made her shiver. A large hand immediately smoothed over her back in response.

"Chenoa?"

Tilting her head back, she forced herself to think. She didn't want to talk, she wanted to feel, simply absorb the way their bodies merged. "Yes, I trust you, Lee."

His mouth captured hers. Lee used his lips to taste her mouth like the finest of wines. His tongue traced her lips before he pulled his head away.

"Completely?"

He seemed intent on his questioning. Chenoa frowned with frustration. She must try to be more clear with her answers so that she could get rid of her dress and his uniform. She did not want to waste the precious hours of the night on conversation. Tomorrow morning she would have to give up their intimacy to reality. But during the night, they could simply be free.

"I would not have bared my breasts for anyone I did not have faith in."

He rubbed her back with that large hand again before stepping away from her. Lee extended his hand toward her with the palm up. "Will you marry me, Chenoa?"

Her breath caught on a harsh note as shock raced across her face. But her hand was already reaching for his out of pure instinct. Chenoa watched Lee close his fingers around her hand. Her mind was frozen with shock yet it simply felt so very right.

Lee didn't give her any further time to consider his question. With her hand firmly held in his he pulled her along with his determined stride.

Chenoa couldn't think of a single bit of her grandmother's advice.

Chapter Nine

Brenda stared at Chenoa with utter shock written across her face the next morning. The modern woman opened her mouth but shut it again as she appeared to consider her words.

Chenoa fought the urge to laugh. She truly didn't understand why such common things were cause for such shock.

"Did you say you got married late night?"

Chenoa nodded her head and laughed anyway. Brenda raised a slim hand and pointed it straight at Chenoa. "To Lee?"

She needed to keep laughing, it kept her from thinking too much. Greeting the sunrise as a wife was threatening to make her into an emotional whirlwind.

Yet there was a solid part of her that was simply content. As if it was something that was fated to be. Chenoa almost snorted in response. If fate were somehow involved it was not the kind of divine intervention a person needed.

Yet Lee had not brought her to the outpost. Inside her heart she sensed the man's honor. So, now she was his wife. Questions were spinning around inside her head. Lee hadn't given her the chance to voice even one of them. A naughty smile crept up her face. She had not been complaining either! Talking seemed to become rather...unimportant when Lee stood close to her.

"It is still rather strange to me. I had never even imagined having a husband."

Chenoa pulled their breakfast from the stove and sat it on the table between them. Her companion was becoming an addict for fresh food. Chenoa was happy to help Brenda with keeping that stinking preserved food out of her body.

"Why would you think that? You are quite pretty. Lots of men must be calling you."

"But there are no men on the Peoples' land. Only boys too young for marriage. The raiders would always be careful to leave the little girls alive and the old women to care for us. But every male child was slaughtered." Chenoa lifted large eyes toward her friend. "It was a very dark time for the people."

Brenda's blue eyes flooded with tears. "Do not hate me, but in my world we dream of a place where there are too many children."

It was like both ways of life were incomplete. One half on the Peoples' land and the other half in the modern man's world. Chenoa snorted with her frustration. "What I hate is that fence."

Brenda blinked away her tears and grinned. "I believe you are right. Finding yourself married must seem like a dream."

"Were you happy to become a wife?"

The question seemed to surprise Brenda. Her blue eyes lit up as she indulged in memories. "I fell for Xan hard. When he asked me to marry him, I think I wore a smile every second of the day 'til I was stupid enough to toss it all away."

Now Chenoa didn't understand. "Did the lieutenant set you aside for another?" She would not have believed it of the fair-eyed man. Chenoa had always sensed honor in the man.

"What? No. I left him."

"Yet you are here. Xan has a pure heart. I have seen his eyes. You should go to him and seek forgiveness. Husbands and wives must forgive each other. That is a need of the marriage vows."

Brenda lifted solemn eyes to Chenoa. "I wish it were that simple but I divorced him. No man would forgive that."

"What is divorce?"

Brenda lifted her hands as if she were explaining the rules of some simple child's game. "I legally ended our marriage."

"Marriage is a binding vow. Once spoken, it is written on your heart. This does not end."

Brenda smiled sadly. "Things aren't so...simple in the real world, Chenoa. Most marriages end in divorce."

Chenoa raised her head as a horrible sensation burned through her stomach. "Lee could do this to me?"

"Well, no one thinks their marriage will end in divorce... But yes...I guess Lee has the right to move on...if he ever wanted to."

That burning sensation turned into full nausea. Chenoa did not understand this world! Move on? When you spoke a promise it was written on your heart. Broken vows haunted you every night even after passing from life into death.

She had given her promise to Lee. There was no moving on for her.

* * * * *

Nacoma was restless. Each second seemed to screech loudly in her ear. Even with the sun setting, the air felt hot. She slipped her sandals on and left her aunt's house. Not sure what she was looking for, she simply walked.

In the dark, the market fountain looked very peaceful. Nacoma kicked her sandals off and playfully kicked at the shimmering water. Her feet became deliciously cool. Loneliness seemed to surround her like a blanket. Nacoma shrugged. She was too sad to fight the emotions tonight.

The night seemed to stretch in front of her with endless hours that were full of long minutes and seconds that would last forever. The blue glow of the fence drew her toward it like a beacon.

Standing close to it, Nacoma felt the slight zing of electricity from it. Her skin rose up into tiny goose bumps. She smiled because it was a feeling. The sensation distracted her from the loneliness.

The glowing blue fence seemed to respond to her. Nacoma narrowed her eyes and watched it shimmer before changing colors. The blue turned lighter as it seemed to develop into waves just like a pond did when a rock was dropped into its center.

The waves rippled out from the center of the light blue area as a hand appeared. Then an arm and a shoulder. A man stood there and pulled his goggles off. Suddenly Nacoma found herself yanked straight out of her tracks and flung away from the newly emerged man.

Another hand was coming through the fence as the large shape of a warrior placed itself between her and the fence. The half moon sent just a tiny amount of light to wash over her protector as he leveled a weapon at the fence. The discharged light beam exploded into the fence.

The waves immediately reversed and traveled back into the center. The arm that was emerging contorted frantically before it was pulled back into the glowing blue field.

"Son of a bitch!"

Her protector's weapon went flying as the first man attacked him. The harsh grunts of battle hit Nacoma's ears as they struggled against each other. But her warrior was far stronger. He brutally flung his attacker away. The man bounced on the ground but was shoved completely down as her warrior efficiently tied his hands behind his back.

The moonlight washed over the harsh cut of the warrior's face as he tied his victim's feet together. He raised his face to the fence to consider the glowing field. A hard nod told Nacoma he found the fence to be secure once again.

"Are you all right?" The moonlight made the competitor into a silver warrior. But Nacoma remembered his voice. Her body suddenly began to tremble and she didn't know why.

"Nacoma?" Kiril stood up and watched her eyes grow as round as saucers. She didn't say a word, not a single sound. But her body was shaking with a violence that frightened him right down to the soles of his boots. What if he'd jerked her too hard? Kiril didn't know exactly how to touch a pregnant woman. Her breath became a harsh rasp that made his alarm spike.

Yanking his jacket off, Kiril wrapped it around her shoulders. Nacoma stiffened slightly before she suddenly burrowed into his embrace. She snuggled right up against his chest and nudged her head into the hollow of his neck.

Nacoma squirmed closer to her warrior's body. They had almost touched her! Out of five missing daughters, only Chenoa had survived. Anyone who went through that fence faced their death. Nacoma wanted to live! Her child needed to live and she had almost been touched by those foul creatures!

But the warm scent of her warrior calmed her. Nacoma sighed blissfully as he wrapped his strong arms about her. She peeked between his arm and chest to where his victim lay on the ground. The man was struggling against his bonds in a frantic attempt to escape.

But Kiril wouldn't let him. Nacoma pulled a deep breath into her body. It was over. This modern man was indeed a warrior with a pure heart. "Thank you."

Kiril felt a ridiculous smile plaster itself across his face. Relief flooded through him leaving him almost weak. Lifting her chin up, he studied her face in the dim light.

"Do you need a doctor?"

Her silvery laughter greeted his ears making Kiril almost giddy. Hell, he'd been smuggled into the competitor ranks just to deal with raiders but seeing their filthy paws so close to Nacoma was almost too much. He'd nearly lost his control to pure blinding rage.

"It would seem that the only person I needed was you." Nacoma moved away from Kiril as she felt her cheeks flush from her boldness. "My thanks, Kiril. I am most grateful you were nearby."

"I was following you."

A wave of energy hit them a second later. It was a harsh collision of plasma particles as a portion of the fence ripped apart from an explosion. The glowing blue surface was sent hurtling out from the center of the fence. Kiril shoved Nacoma to the ground as it burned into their bodies.

The blue particles were still charged and charred their clothing. Kiril rolled both of their bodies across the sand to snuff out flames. His back was screaming with raw pain but he was more concerned about Nacoma.

Looking over his shoulder, Kiril looked at a complete section of the fence that was simply missing. Only the desert night stared back at him. No one was waiting to cross the border. The pirate must have had an explosive on his body. As the fence burned his body away, it had set off the explosion. No amount of explosive could have caused this much damage from outside the fence. But from inside the particle field it had ripped the force field apart.

"I'm burned!" His secured pirate started screaming. Kiril pulled Nacoma from the ground and gently brushed sand off her. He removed his jacket from her. The heavy garment had protected her, as had his own body. In the poor light he couldn't tell exactly how many burns she'd suffered.

"Enforcer, you let me get burned!"

"It's your own fault." Kiril tossed his words out as he considered the immense amount of damage done to the fence. One hundred yards of it were missing. The surrounding scrub brush was either smoldering or still burning. But the explosion had sent the particle material flying into the air with the force of splitting atoms. It was going to rain fire for the next two miles.

"You are an enforcer?" Nacoma stood completely still as she asked the question. Kiril felt himself tense as he delivered his answer.

"Yes."

She smiled that huge smile of hers in response. "Good."

"You like enforcers?"

His voice was coated with doubt making Nacoma laugh again. "I do not like competitors. So it pleases me to know you are not one of those heartless men."

He nodded his huge head a second before the night turned into day. Lights seemed to appear from in front of them. Nacoma raised her hand because such abundance of light made her eyes shrink in protest. Kiril turned abruptly and hauled his captive off the desert floor.

Large vehicles surrounded them as the night became filled with men. They were all warriors like Kiril. Strong and dedicated to their cause. Nacoma watched Kiril as he moved toward his own kind.

He would never come back. Because no one ever came back from outside the fence. Nacoma felt the weight of that truth as it settled onto her shoulders.

"Good work."

"Excuse me, sir?"

Lee turned around and pegged Kiril with his eyes. "I said, good work."

The junior officer tossed his head toward the missing portion of the fence. Lee nodded harshly but held the man's eyes. "Better the fence than another woman. They're getting desperate now." Lee felt his senses tighten. Carrying any kind of explosive through a particle field was asking to get blown up. It was a desperate move by their pirates. They were running out of money. Xan stood looking at the mess before he looked at Kiril next.

"Better let me tend to your back."

"Actually Nacoma needs attention." Kiril turned to look back at the reservation but Nacoma was gone. He searched the sand but could not find her. She wouldn't have run from the enforcers, Kiril was positive of that fact. "I don't understand it. Why did she leave?"

"It's her home, Kiril. Seems rather logical that the girl would choose to seek out her own people for help."

Xan took a confused Kiril toward one of the larger transports. There were reports to file, details to iron out, but he'd caught his pirates. Kiril sat on the tailgate of a transport and grinned as Xan went to work.

Nacoma stared back at him. A curse rolled out of his mouth as Kiril looked straight into the determined eyes of his Indian. She was fifty yards behind the transports, off the reservation. Standing with her arms crossed over her chest.

The young woman's eyes dared anyone to return her to the reservation. She had simply walked around the lights of the transports and not a single enforcer had even thought to keep an eye on her.

Xan let his own curse out as he looked at the Indian woman. Nacoma lifted her face into a huge smile and laughed.

* * * * *

Chenoa watched the compound with a practiced eye now. She knew the different patrols that came and went. She recognized the faces of the men. Their uniforms didn't look the same anymore because she picked out the details that indicated rank and duty assignment.

But the commander wasn't on the compound yet. Her escort was still within eyesight. They held their weapons almost like babies as they talked in low tones. Chenoa missed Kiril. These men were really boys. Their faces were fresh and smooth with youth.

An explosion ripped the night apart. Frantic movement erupted on the compound. Blue streaks flew across the night hitting two of the parked transports. The vehicles lit the night as they began to burn. Men deployed themselves to fight the fire before it spread to the rest of the transports or the compound itself.

Every enforcer on the grounds applied himself to the fight at hand. A column of transports was loaded and moving off into the night even as men rushed to fight the growing fire.

Shouts rose from the men who commanded the efforts. Chenoa fell away from the chaos. A wave of heat hit her in the face as the fire grew even higher. She backed up further. These men were like a well-oiled machine. Each one knew his place and was rushing to take up his post.

Chenoa did not have any place. So she stepped back again and felt the cool night air on her shoulders. She was yanked further into the night by brutal hands that clamped over her mouth and viciously pulled her braids.

"Lookie what I've got." A crude hand groped over her breast. Chenoa violently twisted against her captor. She was shoved to the sand in response. A heavy body landed on top of her as she was roughly gagged.

"Now I've been a really patient boy. Waiting for the time to be just right." Her hands were wrenched in back of her and tied. "Now, it's payday for ol' Dom." A rough hand yanked her feet together as well. "But we're gonna have to take care of this little location beacon first."

The man simply dropped her body. Bound as she was, Chenoa hit the sand with a thud. Her shoulder throbbed with pain. Her ankle exploded in pain next. Dom used a light beam to make the monitor on her ankle destruct. It popped with a flash of blue flame, burning the skin beneath it. Dom snickered as he listened to Chenoa cry through the gag.

"Don't you worry now. I'm going to find you some cock that's got the money to keep you warm and fed." His hand groped for her breast again and pinched her nipple, making nausea rise up her throat. Chenoa frantically tried to control her need to retch. With the gag in place she would choke herself. The groping hand squeezed her belly as he snickered over her body.

"Yo, Dom! Let's go."

He plucked her bound body from the sand and dropped her over his shoulder again. The man began to whistle as he shoved her into the bed of a transport of some kind. It stank of unwashed bodies. Two sets of leering eyes peered at Chenoa over the front seat. One of the men ran a sloppy tongue over his lips. "She's got really plump tits. I ain't never seen tits that plump that were real. Can I squeeze them?"

"Drive, you idiot. That fire isn't big enough to last all night."

The transport jerked into motion making Chenoa strain against her bonds. She was being stolen again. She couldn't endure the separation once more. The skin on her wrists screamed as she twisted and pulled the ropes across the delicate area. Blood made her arms slick and she pulled more.

* * * * *

The enforcer compound was quiet long before Lee finished securing the fence. Chenoa's escort turned toward the commander's housing unit but stood looking for their charge.

"Maybe she's sleeping."

"Yeah, the Commander must keep her up late."

They laughed at the crude idea before two took the rear of the building and two sat on the porch. The leader took out a deck of cards and dealt his buddy in.

She was just an Indian. How much care did she need anyway? The primitives managed to survive in the desert. It seemed like a waste of time to guard her.

* * * * *

Lee surveyed his compound with a critical eye. There was scientific debate over what would actually happen if someone were dumb enough to enter the particle field of the fence with an explosive. But now he had concrete evidence.

It was amazing only the life of the pirate had been lost. Lee didn't waste his time thinking about the deviant. He intended to exterminate every last member of the pirate team.

Chenoa's escort team was itching to be dismissed. They wandered toward him making Lee frown. They were too laid-back for his taste. Half the problem with the outpost was the men that staffed it. Lee had already rotated out a third of the men stationed under his command.

Letting your guard down was asking to get killed. The reason the pirate raids had gotten out of control was the lack of security on the outpost itself. It looked like Lee had a few more men to rotate out of his command.

The one in the lead handed off the monitor unit with a muffled "Sir." Lee felt his collar get tight as a quick look told him the unit was in the off position.

"In case you boys didn't know, these units don't work very well when you turn them off." Lee kept his voice whisper soft. His men snapped to attention in response. Xan and Kiril both appeared with deep frowns marking their faces. The escort visibly paled as they faced the consequences of their sloppy duty.

"Why would you turn it off?" Kiril growled the question. He stepped forward 'til the man in question had to tip his head back to meet his eyes. Anger radiated from the junior officer because these were the men he was responsible for training. Kiril took the lapse of responsibility personally.

"It started chirping during the fire. Every man was needed so..."

Lee slid the switch on the unit to its on position. It let out a shrill alarm that sent him full speed into his home. Xan and Kiril were half a step behind him as they slammed the doors open and searched the structure.

The alarm continued to blare telling them that the unit on Chenoa's ankle wasn't functioning any longer. Ten seconds later, Lee knew it wasn't due to an accident.

His wife was no longer on his compound.

Chapter Ten

Greed did horrible things to a man. Chenoa watched the contorted face of her captor as he eyed the money being offered for her. There was the urgency of a child receiving candy on his face, but displayed on a full-grown man it was pathetic.

His fingers stretched for the money like a starving animal begging for food. His boss enjoyed making him wait. He dangled the money just out of his reach, making her captor stretch his arm even further out.

The depravity of both men made her skin crawl. Being in the same room made Chenoa long for a bath.

Dom squeezed the bundle of money as a twisted smile contorted his face. He never looked at Chenoa as he left the room. He'd sold her. Nausea rose up inside her throat yet again as she stared at human garbage.

Her buyer stood, considering her with bright eyes. He raked her from top to bottom as he critiqued her value. If the gag had not still been over her mouth, Chenoa would have spat on him and his evil.

Instead she was lying on the floor, forced to be his possession. The door swung in as two more men appeared. They were large but coated with fat. Their eyes held that same bright glow of greed.

"Put her in the safe." Chenoa was dragged off the floor by uncaring hands. "And don't damage the merchandise. We got us a real good buyer that ain't paying for bruised fruit."

"Ah hell." Chenoa landed over the man's shoulder and groaned with pain. The sound gained a sharp look from the man who had paid for her.

"I mean it! No bruises and no screwing her either. Dom messed the deal up. We have to unload this girl before the enforcers pick up a trail."

"Got it, Zeik."

The man carrying her walked out the door and through a long hallway. His heavy boots echoed inside the narrow passageway. He passed through doorways and then simply dropped her body. Chenoa hit the hard floor and cried out with the pain. A low snicker was her response.

A rough hand cut the bonds on her arms a second before she was shut into solid darkness. She ripped the gag from her head as she tried desperately to make her eyes work in the pitch-black room.

Pulling the gag off, she worked her jaw up and down. So many hours of being tied up made her body scream. Reaching for her feet, her fingers moved over the knots in slow movements that told her how to untie them. It was a slow process without her eyes.

Chenoa forced herself to draw slow, even breaths into her lungs. Fear would rob her of the ability to think. Her wits were her most important weapon against these animals. She would outsmart them.

But without her sight it wasn't going to be simple. The blackness that surrounded her was complete. It pressed in on her without even a single ray of relief. Stretching her hands out she slowly moved them over the floor. It was rough and cold. Her fingers brushed over dirt.

A wall met her hand so she followed it. The room was big enough to stand in. Light suddenly filled the room as the door reopened. A dull thud hit her ears as a sack hit the floor then the door slammed shut again.

This time there was a small glow of light left in the room. Whatever had been left was glowing a soft green. It was very faint—the light didn't reach the walls. Moving toward it, Chenoa fingered a small glowing tube. It was cool to her touch yet seemed to be glowing from inside. It was no bigger than her thumb.

The sack held food. Thrown inside the rough fabric were vegetables, a crust of bread and a piece of fruit. All tossed together like the kind of meal you would dump into a pig's trough. Her pride reared its head but Chenoa firmly schooled herself to practicality.

The food would give her strength. She could not afford the luxury of pride. Picking up the sack she took the glowing stick around her cell. It was tiny. She could lie down on the floor and touch both walls with her body at the same time. It was not even wide enough to lie across. The walls were concrete blocks but the ceiling seemed to be solid wood.

The pig had called it "the safe". What it was, was a box. A tiny sink sat in a corner. Chenoa felt her mouth beg for water. The faucet looked grimy but worked and a slim stream of water came through its rusty head when she turned the single handle. A foul odor caught her nose and she looked to the floor to find an open pipe. The stench coming from it left no doubt in her mind that this was her only spot for relief.

Sitting her light on the floor, Chenoa rubbed the icy water over her hands and cupped the fluid over her wrists. The skin was blistered and torn. Rubbing at the injuries stung her eyes with tears but she rubbed them more, trying to get as much dirt as possible out of her self-inflicted wounds. If she came down with fever from infection it would weaken her.

Sitting against the far wall, Chenoa forced herself to eat. Her stomach was twisted into a hard knot but she chewed on her meager food and ignored her stiff jaw.

She hated this world.

Tears stung her eyes because she had never hated anything in life before. Her heart ached as she bit into a green bean. It was tasteless, not like the ones she bought at the morning market on the Peoples' land. Mother Earth was right to wipe these people from her face.

The tears fell down her cheeks. She had learned to be so harsh. A hard heart was a bad thing to own. But Chenoa couldn't even hear her grandmother's voice reprimanding her anymore. Her soul was dying in this outside world.

Even Lee did not tell her of his world. Instead he kept her like an exotic pet. Certainly better than her current owner, but not an equal either. Her heart constricted painfully. He was her husband, yet not her partner in life. It made no sense. The way Lee touched her body was so complete but the man was still almost a stranger to her.

And the horrible possibility was, Chenoa might never get the chance to know the man she had pledged her heart to.

* * * * *

Lee felt the hunter inside him shred the other man that civilization demanded he be. He curled his lips back and enjoyed the pure rush. The call to hunt pounded through his body in a primitive tempo.

Chenoa was his!

It was primitive and basic. Lee wanted to choke the life out of the scum that had stolen her. His eyes fell onto the four men of his wife's escort. Sending a glare to his lieutenant, Lee pointed toward the men. "Get those idiots off my outpost."

"With pleasure."

Javier stepped out of the darkness with a harsh look on his face. "Well, Lee. Let's see what kind of trap you managed to design."

It wasn't a jest. Javier's eyes burned with a firestorm that would consume him just as Lee was letting his instincts devour his civilized edge.

Xan and Kiril both caught the scent of blood in the night air and flexed their shoulders. It was the most basic of bonds. Warriors erupted through the layers of discipline as they looked toward the coming hunt.

Only blood would satisfy the hunger and contain the primitive warriors.

* * * * *

Brenda let her mouth hang open. There was no point in trying to close it. Her jaw kept dropping every time she looked in a different direction anyway.

Javier Trey's home took opulence to the extreme. It had to be a sultan's palace. Every angle in the huge, open receiving room flowed. Creamy marble ran across the floor and shimmered as sunbeams streamed in through the windows. Half the ceiling was glass. Huge trees grew inside the hall making the air smell…clean.

Spectacular didn't describe the place. It was decadent.

"You'll need to change. There will be appropriate garments in your rooms." Brenda looked at Javier and shivered. The man was transforming into some sort of predator right in front of her. His voice was brimming full of authority. The kind you didn't cross unless you wanted to pay for the transgression. Looking into his burning eyes, Brenda shivered again because she definitely didn't want to end up on this man's bad side.

"All right." Brenda moved off as she followed a silent servant. The man moved through the marble hallways on feet that didn't seem to touch the floor as he walked. The only sound Brenda heard was her own shoes. In addition there was the soft sound of water flowing and even birds.

Her rooms made her jaw drop again. The guest room was bigger than her entire condo. A fountain bubbled in the center of one room while sweeping gauze was hung from the cathedral ceiling. It all framed the huge bed. The plush bed was set up on a raised portion of the room. You had to walk up five steps to get to it.

"If madam will step this way, please?"

Brenda turned and followed the man. The dressing portion of the rooms was in back of a large garden that was growing inside the room itself. Five mannequins stood with exotic outfits displayed.

"If madam will make her selection."

Her hand flew to her face because the outfits in question all glittered from precious stones that were sewn into them. But there wasn't much fabric. They were cut to expose the female body in all the right spots.

"Um…they're truly stunning but I've got scars on my belly."

"If madam will please wait."

The servant was gone in a second. Brenda strolled around the room absorbing the wonder of it. Her girlfriends would have kicked her in the tail and advised her to make a pass at Javier. The man could certainly keep her in style.

Brenda sighed instead. It was beautiful but, without Xan, she could never love it. She'd take the outpost with its heat in a single second if Xan gave her so much as a wink to encourage her.

"What kind of scars?"

Brenda almost squealed but clamped her jaw together as she spun around. It would seem the servants weren't the only ones who walked silently. But Javier wasn't a man who gave people a head start. He was pure aggression wrapped up in a body that was molded into a solid weapon. He was rumored to be one of the richest men on the planet. Brenda felt herself shiver as she met his eyes. There was something wild looking out of his steel blue eyes. The thing that made her shiver was the fact that Javier didn't try to hide that inner beast. Instead he embraced it.

Brenda pulled her shirt up to simply let the man judge for himself. Reconstructive surgery had left her with long dark scars. But the surgery hadn't been an option. The only form of birth control that wasn't illegal was abstinence. Even something like failing to have her damaged fallopian tubes repaired would have been an offence punishable by a prison sentence. The stunning outfits he'd wanted her to wear were all bare across the midsection.

"Excellent. They'll make our cover more complete. Wear the blue one. The scars will show better."

Letting her shirt fall back down, Brenda slowly shook her head. "I guess I should have thought about that." They were trying to buy a fertile woman to bear their child. The scars on her body would lend testimony to their previous efforts.

Javier considered her for a moment. That shiver crossed her again as he slowly circled her on silent steps. Brenda followed him with her eyes. The man reminded her of a panther she'd once watched at the zoo.

"These flesh traders think you belong to me." It was a statement. The man continued to circle her in a slowly decreasing stride. One hand landed on her arm and she jumped. He laughed low in his chest and raised a single finger up in reprimand.

Brenda smiled and Javier slid his hand over her shoulder in a smooth movement that declared his ownership. Brenda simply let him touch her. The truth was, the touch didn't really bother her. It also didn't excite her.

"Well, I guess Xan is a lucky man."

"What do you mean?"

Javier crossed his arms over his chest as he studied her body with deep consideration. A grin lifted his lips as he returned to her eyes and found her staring at him with curiosity and nothing more.

"Most women would at least fake some interest in me, if for nothing else but my money. It's rather refreshing to see that your love isn't for sale. Xan is rich beyond measure to have you."

Brenda watched the man stride from the room. Oddly enough, she laughed. She was a modern woman but really quite ignorant. Javier had absolutely everything in the world worth having but he was incomplete. It was strange to see one of the world's most powerful men looking lonely.

But she understood. Even a palace was just a place without love. Maybe that was why the man seemed to embrace his inner beast. The women who pursued him were relentless and all that did was leave him empty.

Brenda found herself considering the man that half the women in the world were chasing for his fortune. In their minds, he was an object. The key to their future. The same world labeled Chenoa the same way. She was a fertile vessel. But she was also a person.

Brenda pulled the blue skirt from the mannequin with firm purpose. The dress form was a hologram and it released the garment with a golden flicker. Chenoa was her friend. Brenda was going to enjoy watching these animals get caught.

They were giving the human race a foul name.

* * * * *

Waiting was an art.

Lee felt the familiar tension as he waited for his trap to close. But tonight it wasn't the comfortable sensation he was accustomed to. His pride didn't seem willing to lend him confidence in his plan.

Lee let a low growl roll out of his chest. Emotional evolvement with anything led to distraction. Each little hiccup in the plan made his body tense just a little bit more. Javier strode back into the room.

"She getting ready?" His words came out in a snarl but Lee didn't care. He wasn't in the mood to be cordial. He wanted his wife back.

"Waiting is an implement of the devil."

Javier laughed as Lee simply frowned deeper. "Love, however, is proof that God has a sense of humor."

"Who said I'm in love?"

Javier lifted a crystal glass to his lips. Eighty-year-old Scotch burned his mouth with just the right amount of sting. "Your face says it, my friend."

Lee lifted an eyebrow in response. Love wasn't a word that he'd taken a whole lot of notice of in his life. It was an outdated label. A primitive means of binding a mate to you.

"You're a stubborn man, Lee."

Well, that much was true. Lee lifted a glass of Scotch and simply swirled the liquor around the edge of the glass. He certainly felt a great number of things for Chenoa. But love was a mysterious thing that drove people to lifelong commitments.

Lee suddenly laughed. He raised his Scotch in a salute to Javier before he tossed the drink into his mouth. "God must be having a good laugh today, because you are annoyingly correct about too many things."

Lee wasn't sure about love but he was completely convinced that Chenoa belonged to him. The thing that made it all so funny was the plain fact that he was chained to Chenoa. There was an unbreakable bond that connected him to her. Lee would search for her until death took him away from the planet. He wouldn't think about a life that didn't include his wife. The truth was…he belonged to Chenoa.

If that was love, he was in it.

* * * * *

Her prison was silent. So quiet, Chenoa found herself listening to the beat of her own heart. When the door was pulled open it was an explosion of sound, almost deafening with its sheer volume.

"You idiot! She's shivering! If the boss finds out he'll carve your cock off with a steak knife."

"It's just a Indian."

Chenoa kept her temper tightly leashed. One of the men came toward her with his hand outstretched. His tense body told her he half expected her to fly into his face like some kind of terrorized animal.

Their ignorance might just work to her advantage. Chenoa kept her mouth shut as he pulled her from the concrete cell. She shuffled her feet slightly, but allowed the man to pull her along a hallway. Every step she took from that cell increased her odds of escape.

"So now what, genius?"

The man escorting her stopped inside a rather small bathroom. His companion tugged on his hair as he tried to decide just what to do. Her arm was released as the first man flipped the shower on. He grabbed her hand and stuck it under the falling water.

"You're an idiot, Eric. Does she smell like she doesn't know how to bathe?"

"That don't mean she'll take a shower."

The first man turned Chenoa toward the running water. She kept her face blank. Pointing to the door she firmly ordered them to leave. The first man laughed at his companion.

"See. She understands just fine."

"So the savage knows what a shower is. Big deal," Eric grumbled as he went back into the hallway. Chenoa felt hope spring up inside her but clamped her lips together to contain it. She mustn't let them even suspect she understood their language.

The first man lingered in the bathroom. Indecision was written on his face. Chenoa frantically tried to think of how to get him to leave her alone. She stuck her hand into the water and splashed it toward her body. Nodding her head she used her other hand to grasp the front of her dress tightly closed. Her jailer smiled showing chipped teeth.

"Shy, huh? Okay, but old Frank is gonna be right outside this here door."

Chenoa let her smile lift her face. She clamped her jaw shut on the laughter that went with the smile. The door shut with a solid click. She watched it with a critical eye before turning to face the small window above the shower.

Chenoa wasn't even sure the men had seen the window. It was at the top of the shower stall in the back. Thin and long, she might just be able to slip through it. Grabbing a stool she climbed up to look at her one opportunity for escape. The water immediately soaked half her body but she didn't dare to turn it off.

The latch was coated with rust but Chenoa forced it to release. The wind hit her face and she smiled again. The pigs that held her were so stupid. On the Peoples' land, the body must be strong. Chenoa had spent her childhood climbing. She spent her adulthood working with the members of her tribe. She was strong and pushed the window open before she used her arms to pull her body up to the opening.

Slipping her feet through the open window, Chenoa didn't bother to look at what she would drop into. She didn't care. Escape would be worth landing on a bed of cactus.

Instead she dropped into the most foul-smelling mud. Pushing to her feet, Chenoa considered the dark alleyway. The buildings were built with barely two feet between them. The sun never penetrated the spot and it stank of infected water.

Chenoa stared in fascination at the opening in front of the building. People walked by. Many people. Transports moved past but they were much smaller than the one Lee used on his compound. These were brightly colored with one or two people inside them. Chenoa moved toward the opening on cautious steps. She peeked out at the people but no one looked at her.

In fact, they didn't look at each other either. The people on the street scurried past each other and averted their eyes. There was no greeting, not even a smile or nod. Young men cut in front of elderly women without a single care. One old woman was slowly dragging a heavy cart along with her. A group of three men came up behind her and wove around her. Not a single one of them offered to ease her burden. They did not even greet her. The old woman didn't seem to expect it either. She simply continued to pull her burden alone.

What a shameful world. Chenoa swallowed her anger because the callous disregard surrounding her was also allowing her to escape. She stepped onto the walkway and joined the flow of people.

No one noticed her. No one even looked at her. Chenoa curled her lips back with revulsion. She picked up her pace because she felt the need for distance. In the crowd of uncaring people she would become just another faceless human.

The callous indifference was becoming her salvation. Keeping her eyes moving, Chenoa searched the streets for an enforcer's uniform. It was the only plan she could come up with. So she walked and searched, silently praying her husband was searching for her as well.

Even in the stream of people, Chenoa heard her captors coming for her. She fought against the urge to run. Casting a look behind her, she saw Eric yanking women around to face him as he thundered along the sidewalk. Panic screamed along her body but Chenoa held onto her composure.

The second she bolted they would run her down like a rabbit.

Considering the speed of Eric's approach, Chenoa turned and ducked into a doorway. Her lungs screamed as she tried to breathe in a thick cloud of smoke. She could see it floating at eye level in a thin cloud. Her eyes went wide as she took in the sour-smelling place—there were tables and chairs all in different configurations. Men were at the tables—some were playing a card game of some sort, many were watching the game. They were all holding large cups of amber colored drink that they would take huge swallows from and wipe their mouths on their sleeves.

"Hey, pretty, let me buy you a beer."

Whistles and cheers accompanied the invitation. A meaty hand gripped her arm and what looked to be the owner of the crude place raked her with harsh eyes. He leaned down close to her ear.

"You hook in my place, I get a cut. Clear?" Chenoa nodded her head just to appease the man. She didn't know what he meant but she needed the crowd of loud men to hide in. They might be rude but they weren't out to sell her. The owner immediately smiled as she agreed with him. "Well, now maybe we can work a little arrangement out. Get your tail over there and make those boys drink." He settled his eyes over her breasts as his tongue took a swipe at his lips. "Go on. Don't take less than a hundred. I get half."

Chenoa did as she was told. The men welcomed her with low whistles and bold eyes that traveled down her body. Chenoa aimed her eyes at the game. The men resumed it with vigor.

The owner arrived with a tray of drinks. The men hooted and greedily reached for the beverages. They tossed coins onto the tray, making the owner chuckle. A hand snaked around her waist and pulled Chenoa onto a lap. She squirmed but the owner shot her a deadly glance. "I'm gonna buy you a drink, sweet thing."

More coins landed on the tray as the owner smirked at her. The man returned to his game with Chenoa on his lap. Precious minutes ticked by. Chenoa could only pray Eric was making his way away from her hiding place.

* * * * *

Lee enjoyed being in control. It might be prideful but it was true. He felt a surge of adrenaline hit his bloodstream before he'd even cleared the door of Javier's house. A good strategist never left a detail to chance.

Lee was one of the best.

Few spots in the city were as seedy as Parker's Corner. It was also one of the most likely spots for the black market to use as storehouse for their goods. It had been a good bet to post a few men around the area.

Guilt arrived right on the heels of that adrenaline. Lee should have taught Chenoa a little bit about his world. There was a call terminal on every street corner. She'd walked right by the small palm-activated communication devices. Her handprint would have given instant access to a communications grid. By giving the machine his name, a call would have instantly come through on his communicator.

Instead his wife was walking down one of the roughest streets in the city with slave traders on her heels.

Lee tightened his nerve. He couldn't think about the half dozen ways Chenoa might end up dead in the fourteen minutes it would take him to reach her. The local enforcer commander was pleased to report that he had the area down to one murder per day.

* * * * *

"Let's go have some fun."

Chenoa succeeded in getting off the man's lap this time. He bolted up from his chair and licked his lips as his eyes dropped to her breasts. "Come here, sweet thing. I'm going to make you dance." He thrust his hips forward in vulgar movements. His companions hooted with laughter. One even landed a hard smack onto her bottom.

Chenoa spun on her heel and darted past the intoxicated group. Her haven had become too dangerous to remain in. She scurried toward the door but the owner caught her arm and dragged her to a halt.

"We had us a deal, girl."

Chenoa looked at the familiar twist of greed on this man's face. Did these people in the outside world think of nothing but money? The laughter behind her became louder as the men shoved their chairs back in order to chase her. Chenoa frantically considered the owner and his rough grip on her arm.

"He did not pay. You wanted money but he said he would give me none."

"What's that?" The angry eyes of the owner immediately shifted to the group of men. He shoved Chenoa roughly behind him as he went to take issue with the men. His greedy voice echoed off the grimy walls of the place.

"The girl says you didn't pay. What sort of place do you think I run?"

Grateful for the opportunity, Chenoa turned toward the door and froze. Eric snickered in a sickening voice as he flexed his fingers. Caught between the two men, Chenoa wasn't sure which fate was worse.

The only thing she was certain of was the fact that her luck had completely run dry.

Chapter Eleven

"Think you're real smart, don't you?" Eric stepped forward and caged Chenoa inside with his huge body. "Frank's mama was an Indian bitch so he's soft. Maybe I'll just make a little extra money off you right here for my trouble. These boys will pay to jump between your thighs and I don't see as how it makes much difference. Zeik will be selling your cunt to some other fellow tonight."

Chenoa felt the blood drain from her face. Eric's eyes were twisted with greed. His face was contorted with vengeance. This man had no heart. He snickered again and sucked in a gasp of air. His face suddenly became frozen, the features unmoving as his eyes lost their light and he fell to the floor in a heap.

A booted foot shoved his sprawled body out of the doorway. Her husband's eyes were glowing with primal rage as he looked at his victim.

"Hey, she's ours!"

Lee snaked an arm around Chenoa and her feet left the ground. Her husband's familiar strength made her tremble as relief stole every last ounce of composure Chenoa had left. He dropped her behind him and used his massive body to shield her from the group stalking her.

"The lady's got a prior commitment." Lee slowly backed out of the bar. If they wanted a fight, he'd be glad to indulge them. Just not in the doorframe. "Chenoa, get into the transport."

A large hand gripped her shoulder and pulled her backwards away from Lee. Chenoa was pushed behind the large shoulders of Xan as he moved up next to her husband. A third pair of hands gripped her shoulders in a firm hold. Chenoa looked into the serious eyes of Kiril as he moved her behind his body.

Kiril watched her 'til she'd sat down in the open door of their transport. He sent the enforcers inside a harsh look before he turned to join Lee and Xan. They'd backed up onto the sidewalk but men were spilling out of the doorway. The men challenging the enforcers should have taken a moment to notice just how enraged the three men were.

The first man to attack ended in a pile at her husband's feet. Chenoa simply watched his shoulders as Lee applied his strength to defending himself. It was a very harsh fact of life. But Chenoa found her eyes glued to her mate as he insisted on standing in front of her.

A wave of fatigue hit her suddenly. Chenoa felt her head roll back and hit the seat back. Goose bumps rose up all along her skin as she became so cold her teeth began to chatter. The young enforcer next to her aimed horrified eyes at her but Chenoa didn't know why.

She was so very tired! In her entire life, Chenoa didn't think she had ever felt so completely exhausted. The sounds that surrounded her became soft and distant. Chenoa sighed because it made it easier to rest. But she fought the pull of sleep because she wanted Lee. Just wanted to touch him. Assure herself that he was truly there.

The fight didn't take much of the edge off of Lee's appetite. He hauled Eric's unconscious form from the pub before they quit the area. The intoxicated rats from the pub were all scurrying away. His communications unit chimed for attention. Lee jerked the thing off his arm and growled into it.

"Tanner."

"The meeting is still on." Javier's voice was furious. Flat and frozen with his rage, Javier Trey hated anyone trying to play him for a fool.

"Excellent. I'm inbound now." Lee felt his lips lift into a small smile. One more pirate was walking right into his trap.

Most importantly, that was one less scumbag that would be eyeing his fence.

Turning his eyes onto his wife, Lee felt his stomach drop. She was pasty white. Her body looked far too frail as it shook. Slipping into the seat, Lee gathered her against his chest. Relief surged through him as her familiar scent reached his senses. Xan pressed her shoulders toward Lee as the lieutenant kept pressing 'til Chenoa was sandwiched tightly between their larger bodies. It was the best treatment for shock they had at their disposal.

Lifting his wrist, Lee typed in a message to Javier. They had Chenoa back and it was time to tie up the loose ends. Lee didn't spare much sympathy for Zeik. Anyone who tried to steel from Javier ended up facing the demon that the man was often accused of being.

* * * * *

Some people had too much. Zeik almost sneered but stopped himself before the emotion crossed his face.

Javier saw it anyway. But in Zeik's case, he didn't need to see anything on the man's face. The vermin reeked of his greed. Toying with one of Brenda's curls, Javier deliberately drew out the meeting. Men like Zeik were good at avoiding traps. That made it all so much more interesting to hunt them.

Pushing a line of code into his terminal, Javier transferred money into Zeik's account. The rodent's eyes bulged forward as he looked at his own terminal. But he squinted and frowned a moment later.

"That's only half."

"Do I look like a fool?" Javier used a finger to tip Brenda's head up to his. She was grateful for the reprieve from Zeik's harsh scrutiny. "You must think I'm an idiot."

"Now I didn't say that." Zeik shifted his body from foot to foot in agitation.

"Good. You will now produce the merchandise."

Zeik put on his best smile. He had been hoping to get all the money but, well, he wasn't going to complain. It was still a bloody fortune. It was sure too bad that things were getting too hot in the Indian selling business. But it was time to be moving on. Just enough time to fleece this last fat sheep.

"I'll go arrange for the delivery."

Javier waited for Zeik to turn and walk away from him. The man's shoulders were just relaxing when he pushed to his feet and jumped toward the man. Zeik didn't even turn around. Brenda watched in silent awe as he sent Zeik into the marble floor with a blow that was silent and fluid.

There was a harsh sound of metal on metal as Javier reached for one of the wall decorations. The man pulled a rapier from its scabbard and held the very real weapon exactly on Zeik's throat.

"Due to a rather ironic twist of fate, there isn't an enforcer close enough to save your miserable life." Zeik choked as Javier used the tip of his weapon to open a wound on the man's exposed belly.

"Don't kill me! I know stuff. Lots of stuff."

The rapier flashed through the air to stop right above Zeik's throat again. Brenda watched as Javier's eyes began to almost glow. He curled his lips back 'til his teeth showed like fangs. "My mother was an Amish woman. A cockroach like you sold her to a bastard like my father."

Zeik's eyes bulged wide a second before Javier thrust the slim blade into his shoulder. The pirate screamed, pinned to the floor by the blade. Javier's eyes watched the man's agony before he left him and settled back into his comfortable spot to await the arrival of the enforcers. There wasn't a hint of remorse in Javier's eyes for Zeik's suffering.

Instead Brenda was certain she saw the bright flame of justice burning for the woman who had born him.

* * * * *

Nacoma propped her hands onto her hips, making her belly stick out even further. Her eyes were snapping black fire and Kiril swallowed roughly. He'd rather face a laser rifle bare-handed than this.

"I will see Chenoa."

Kiril stretched his arms wide. Nacoma studied his stance as she tried to decide how to get around him and into the commander's quarters. The woman wouldn't listen to orders. But Kiril didn't have that luxury. The commander had ordered him to keep Nacoma away from Chenoa. The order was becoming one of the biggest feats Kiril had ever undertaken.

"Chenoa is sick."

"Just a cold."

"You're pregnant."

Nacoma hissed at him. "I have noticed that I am pregnant! It does not mean I am useless. But I waste my breath explaining this to a man!"

A large transport glided into the compound capturing Nacoma's attention. Kiril ran a hand through his hair in agitation. At least Nacoma was interested in their visitors. He needed the break!

Chenoa laughed at the junior officer just before she gave in to another coughing fit. Nausea accompanied the cough but there was nothing in her stomach. Chenoa was certain of that fact!

She was positively miserable.

At least there was no fever. Chenoa went back to her bed and flopped down on her back. Her stomach knotted and cramped. Sitting for hours in that cold cell had taken its toll on her body. She was grateful she wasn't sicker.

Her eyes focused on the bottle of Gyseratel sitting beside her bed. Lee was insisting she take the immune system booster. But she was going to have to be much sicker to endure the stench of the drug. Her husband wasn't dealing with her refusal very well.

Chenoa laughed again. Actually, her husband was quite angry. She looked at the two capsules he'd laid out for her and considered tossing them down the plumbing. It would save her the trouble of dealing with Lee's displeasure.

Chenoa rolled over instead. Becoming dishonest wasn't the answer. Lee was her husband and she must learn to deal with him. In this case, he would be the one learning that she would not stink just because of a little cold.

Letting her eyes close, Chenoa let her mind rest. In so many ways she was still lost. It was truly strange the way life could suddenly change so very dramatically. Everything she had ever known about life meant nothing outside the Peoples' land.

She still felt so blind, very much like the day she'd first awakened in the enforcer's station. A small smile crossed her face. Lee's voice still made her tremble too.

Men were rather complex. Chenoa did not understand many of Lee's words. But what she found most confusing was the way none of her thinking mattered when the man touched her. There was a current that swept her into its deep waters. Strangely enough, she went willingly to the bottom of the stream. It was almost like she belonged there, with Lee.

She must rest and get well. Nacoma would help her understand. They had been best friends since the cradle. Another woman would help her understand the tangle of emotions that seemed to be crushing her. Besides, Chenoa didn't want Kiril to end up an aged man before his time.

* * * * *

Brenda actually stomped her foot with outrage. She'd never thought people actually did that except in books. The desert sand didn't give her an ounce of satisfaction either.

Javier smirked at her temper. And then the man kissed her.

Brenda squealed as he pulled her against his body and covered her mouth with firm unrelenting lips. He thrust past her outrage to take a deep taste of her mouth. He lingered over the touch, savoring the intimacy.

"Goodbye, Brenda."

"You're despicable!" Brenda hissed her reply but quickly stepped out of the man's reach. He smiled again before swinging up into his transport's front seat. The driver immediately engaged the drive system. Javier firmly closed the door, leaving her standing on the compound and waiting on Xan to allow her to leave it again.

Brenda snorted softly. Well, at least she was sitting at rock bottom. It just couldn't get any worse than this.

A hard hand spun her around and yanked her next to the unyielding strength of her ex-husband. His hand captured her head and tipped it up to meet the furious glare coming from his blue eyes.

Xan's face was etched with anger. "Are you lovers?"

Brenda blinked her eyes in shock. That almost sounded like jealousy. Her heart jumped at the sign of Xan's affection for her. "No. I don't know why he kissed me." Brenda melted against Xan. She wanted to savor the moment she had to be next to him, surrounded by his strength. Her body leapt in response, her nipples rising up into tight little buds. His breath caught on a harsh note as he rubbed his chest against her, a slow movement that made her gasp with sensation.

"I guess I know why he kissed you." Xan watched confusion cross Brenda's face as he gave her a half smile. "Let's not let his matchmaking efforts go to waste."

Xan closed a hand over her wrist and turned toward the opposite end of the housing compound. Brenda followed with her thoughts still spinning. Matchmaking? Xan didn't miss a beat. Instead her ex-husband shoved open the door to his quarters and pulled her back into his embrace as the door swung shut again.

He captured her mouth in a kiss that turned her knees to liquid. He caught the moan that escaped her as he thrust his tongue into her mouth to boldly remind her just how a man kissed his wife. It was determined and relentless.

And most importantly…it was Xan.

* * * * *

Her husband was not pleased.

Chenoa grinned. The two capsules of Gyseratel were being tossed up and down in his palm. An irresistible urge to be naughty and pull his tail erupted inside her. Chenoa wanted to erase the stern look sitting on his face.

Rolling over, she came up onto her knees with a pillow in her hands. Swinging it at her husband, Chenoa was rewarded with a soft woof as it hit him right across his face. Her weapon was plucked from her fingers a second later to end up flying over her head and right back onto the bed.

Lee abruptly halted as he looked at his wife. Completely bare, she thrust her breasts out proudly as she smiled up into his eyes. She was truly magnificent. Emotion erupted inside him in a furious stream. Lee inspected her body from head to toe as he felt the burn of possession hit him.

Chenoa felt her smile fade. The heat of her husband's raptor eyes melted all traces of silliness from her. Her blood began to race as she considered being reunited with her warrior. Her breasts lifted under his eyes.

Lee felt a smile lift a corner of his mouth as he tossed the Gyseratel back onto the bedside table. "You're very stubborn, Mrs. Tanner."

"You are too used to giving orders, Husband. I am not one of your men."

"I've noticed that." Lee landed on the bed beside her and ran a soft tongue over a nipple. Chenoa gasped and he gripped her waist to turn her to face him. Licking the soft tip of her breast again he sucked it firmly into his mouth. "In fact, I'm really enjoying the differences between you and my men."

His lips wandered over to her opposite nipple and pulled it into his mouth. Chenoa threaded her fingers through his hair as she offered her breasts up for his attention. Heat snaked down from the touch right into her belly. Need blossomed into a raging inferno as Lee trailed his kisses down the soft skin of her stomach.

He wanted to taste her. Immerse himself in her scent. Maybe it was some primitive need still lurking in the back of his brain but Lee intended to mark every last inch of her flesh with his mouth.

Chenoa felt the determination of her partner. Excitement coiled in her breast as she felt his grip become solid. Lee raised his face to display the intense glow of his hawk's eyes to her. There was a need burning inside those orbs that made Chenoa toss her head.

"Lay back." Her pride reared its head but it seemed to excite Lee even more. He didn't want mere coupling from her. Tonight, her warrior wanted her to surrender to him.

"I want to taste you." Her pride lost in a second as Chenoa recalled in vivid detail the night he'd tasted her on the table. A deep shudder shook her as she collapsed back onto the bed. Lee growled in a low rumble that made her shudder again. This time it was in anticipation.

"Good. Now open your legs for me. Show me what you want me to taste."

She raised her knees and parted them to expose her sex to his stare. Lee growled again as he enjoyed the pure rush of sensation that hit him as her delicate folds fell open. His sex was painfully hard with need. He savored the feeling as he considered denying the raging need to mate in order to hear his mate cry out in rapture. He wanted to make her scream.

Rubbing a hand over her breast again, Lee gently squeezed the flesh as Chenoa's body moved in delicate shivers. Moving down he stroked her soft abdomen and listened to her breath catch. Her thighs were coated in firm muscle, which made him growl in approval.

"Lift your breasts for me." Chenoa lifted liquid eyes to his. Lee stilled over her belly and waited. He could smell the heavy scent of her arousal as he waited for complete compliance.

Chenoa found her will was bound to his in some primitive manner. All she felt was raging need. He smiled as she cupped her breasts toward his mouth. His tongue lapped each rosy peak before sucking it into his mouth. A single finger dove into the moist center of her body, rubbing against her woman's bud, making it pulse.

He dropped his head to her exposed sex and her head fell back. A sharp cry escaped her lips as his tongue found her center. He licked along the sensitive folds 'til he stopped to nuzzle at her most sensitive spot. As he sucked the nub into his mouth, Chenoa let another cry escape her lips as her body exploded in a shower of sensation.

She came too quickly. Lee sucked her sex into his mouth and began building the sensation again. Full of her scent, he used his tongue to firmly bring her back to aching need. Her hips jerked up, offering her body to his mouth. His sex was throbbing with need as her cries became sharp again. Her body released a second orgasm that left his wife panting. Lee raised his head to devour the sight of his mate sprawled on his bed. It made his body coil into tight aggression.

The way he rose over her body made Chenoa shiver. He was almost more myth than man in that instant, an ancient warrior who had claimed her as his mate. He rolled over and took her with him. His shoulders ended up flat on the bed and his hands guided her thighs around his hips.

"Ride me." His voice was a hard order born from need. The hard thrust of his erection rose straight up from his abdomen as his hands gripped her hips and lifted her over its swollen thrust.

"I want to watch you take me."

Chenoa shivered at the image. She'd always been beneath his powerful body. The hard tip of his weapon probed for entry as he began to lower her onto its length. Her body rejoiced at the penetration and she tightened her thighs around his hips to control her own body weight. Her body rejoiced as she impaled herself on his hard flesh.

"Now lift your bottom."

She rose off him and his hands pushed her back down immediately. His eyes were glued to sight of his penetration and she rose once more as she watched his face glow with primitive enjoyment. His hand shoved her down and she lifted just as quickly. Deep pleasure flowed though her body as she moved faster.

She was magnificent. Lee groaned as she sunk down on his length and then felt his body buck under her weight before she lifted her hot passage off him. Her breasts bounced with the motion as he reached for one of the mounds and pinched the nipple. Her thighs gripped him tighter as she rose and fell with greater urgency.

"That's it honey, faster."

She had never enjoyed his orders so much! Leaning over his chest she let her breasts hang towards him. Pleasure knotted in her womb as she forced her legs to move her faster.

Her eyes flew open as she listened to the harsh sounds of fulfillment come from her lover. Lee's face was cut into angles of primitive need as he gripped her hips for his release. His seed hit her womb and Chenoa cried out with him as her body tightened around his, pulling and gripping his rod to capture his seed.

She collapsed onto Lee, his arm holding her against his chest as they both labored for breath. Chenoa ran her fingers along the sculpted perfection of his shoulders. His eyes sank into hers and she shivered again. Dominance of any kind was completely missing. Instead her husband's golden brown eyes looked into her with a longing that swore allegiance to her.

It was a brief moment of exposure, which her husband ended by rolling her onto his side. His hands lifted her body and arranged it along his as he stroked her with firm hands.

Chenoa laid her head along his heart and listened to its beat. Her heart was bursting with joy. It had always been this way between them. Maybe someday her husband would learn to speak the words that were written in his eyes.

* * * * *

"Chenoa?"

The sound of her husband's voice made her jump. Chenoa rubbed her head and climbed slowly to her feet. She'd been appreciating the fact that Lee would leave the house before sunrise. That way he missed her morning nausea.

All other symptoms of her cold were gone and Chenoa didn't think that a little nausea was reason to confine her back to bed. Smoothing a hand over her hair she opened the bathroom door.

"Are you all right?"

Chenoa nodded her head but Lee gave her a suspicious look anyway. Chenoa lifted her chin and pressed her lips into a firm line. Maybe it was good her husband was here in the bright light of day. It was time for him to stop treating her like a wounded dove.

"What I need is some work. Nacoma and I are going to begin planting a garden today."

"Nacoma will rest."

Chenoa set her shoulders. "That would be foolish. The work will ease her labor. Her time is close."

"The doctors are advising bed rest."

Chenoa shook her head. "What could men know of such things? To be a burden on your people is a shame."

The way Chenoa made things sound so simple deflated Lee's arguments. Watching Brenda try to keep up with the two

Indian women drove home the fact that Chenoa was completely at home in the desert. She and Nacoma were both very adept at living in the environment. Considering the way Chenoa seemed to glow with health, maybe he should let them plant their garden.

Besides, he had another battle to fight with his wife. One Lee wasn't willing to accept defeat over. "All right, but if Nacoma has any problem you will promise me you'll contact Xan?"

Chenoa nodded her head. Lee set his shoulders before he raised his hand to display a tracking unit. Chenoa's eyes registered immediate recognition. Her lips pressed tightly together as she glared at the thing. Lee ground his teeth together and waited.

"Chenoa, I don't want to have to put this on you again."

Yet he would use his strength to see the thing strapped onto her body if she refused. Chenoa saw determination glittering in his eyes. But he was asking her. There was a vast difference today from the first time he'd ordered her to wear the ankle band.

Lee watched her eyes and waited. Defiance wasn't flashing from her face. It was better than he'd expected. No matter what her feelings, Lee wasn't leaving until her protection had been seen to. "I won't take the chance with your safety. Sit down." Her eyes did flash and Lee held them. "Please."

That one word was a concession. Chenoa lost her determination as her husband locked his jaw in anticipation of battling with her. Somehow the idea that he liked the idea as little as she did made it somewhat bearable.

Dropping her body to their bed she lifted one leg up to the surface of the bed as well. But Chenoa raised her left leg instead of her right one. Deep burns were still healing along her right ankle from the first monitor that had been secured there.

"Marriage is learning to walk as one soul."

Her grandmother's voice floated across her ears again. Chenoa smiled faintly with the memory even as Lee tightened the monitor on her ankle. He stroked the side of her face with a warm hand before turning toward the door.

Compromising had pleased him. Chenoa chewed her lip as she considered if it was worth wearing the black monitor on her body. Raising her opposite leg she considered the burns marring her skin.

Chenoa knew the dangers of the desert well. Yet she knew close to nothing about Lee's world. The greed that poisoned its people was so very hard for her to understand. But she had felt its claws upon her body.

Standing up, Chenoa went to find Nacoma. She could not waste the day worrying about things that could not be changed.

Chapter Twelve

"You promised me!"

Her husband's temper made Chenoa snap her head around to glare at him. Nacoma hissed under her breath, making Chenoa angrier.

"Why do you yell at me?"

Lee stomped forward but skidded to a halt as his eyes fell onto Nacoma. His eyes grew wide as he pointed at Chenoa. "You promised you would contact Xan."

Chenoa searched her memory but she had little time for her husband. His words reminded her of their conversation. "There is no problem. Your lieutenant has no reason to be here."

"She's having that baby!"

Nacoma hissed again as she tried to keep her attention on her labor. Chenoa whipped around and pushed her husband out of the tiny housing unit that Kiril had relinquished to Nacoma. Lee went willingly enough. The idea of delivering a baby scared him to death.

"I have delivered many babies."

"You have?"

"Yes. There is great need of midwives on the Peoples' land. I have studied this for many years." Chenoa turned around and returned her attention to Nacoma. Chenoa giggled as her friend stuck her tongue out at Lee. Brenda laughed and tried to hide her smile behind her hand.

Casting her eyes about, Chenoa made certain everything was ready. Xan had provided everything she needed to help Nacoma deliver the child. But the best method was to simply let nature take its course.

Chenoa would not interfere unless the baby's heart rate slowed. A tiny monitor was attached to Nacoma.

Lee snorted as he listened to the laughter through the closed door. Xan echoed the sound.

"How can they be laughing?" Lee looked at the door but backed away instead. He didn't need to know right now. Maybe tomorrow, after that baby had been born. He frowned as he considered the closed door again.

"How long does it take for a baby to be born?"

Xan tossed his hands into the air. "Every birth is different. It could take days."

Ah...*hell.*

Three hours later, the woman began singing. They laughed at their own mismatched harmony and giggled some more. In fact, it seemed like they were attempting to be louder with each outburst.

Lee looked at his two junior officers and cussed. Kiril followed suit and Xan pulled at his hair some more. The ground was packed firm from their boots pacing across it. A thin cry came from the cabin and made Lee freeze. It was too low to be one of the women. It reminded him of a kitten.

Seconds crawled by when nothing but silence remained. An entire hour passed before the door finally opened. Chenoa raised her finger to her lips, warning them to be quiet. She and Brenda slipped out of the cabin on silent feet.

Raising a hand to her hair, Chenoa rubbed her forehead. She was tired. Yet it was a good fatigue that came from a labor of love. A small smile lifted her lips as she felt her heart rejoicing. It was good to be needed.

Lee and his officers looked at her with haggard faces. Chenoa blinked her eyes and looked again to make certain she wasn't more tired than she believed. All three men looked at her with deeply worried eyes.

"What is wrong?" Something horrible must have happened on the compound while she had been with Nacoma for Lee and his officers to look so...frantic.

Kiril lunged forward, stopping a mere foot in front of her body. "Something's wrong? What?"

The junior officer nearly roared his demand. Chenoa planted her hands on the man's chest and shoved him away from the housing unit. "Shh. Nacoma is sleeping. What has happened out here?"

"Out here? Nothing happened out here!" Kiril flung his arms into the night as he paced in a circle before aiming pleading eyes back at Chenoa. "What about the baby?"

Chenoa smiled. "Nacoma has a fine daughter. She has named her Tadi."

The three men shook with relief, making Chenoa frown. "Do you mean that you have all been here worrying?"

"Hell, yes!"

Lee growled the response and his wife laughed. Amusement lit up her eyes as she surveyed him.

Brenda smothered a giggle herself. "I guess you didn't tell them the rules."

"It is not a rule." Chenoa looked at her companions and shook her head. Truly, she did not understand such ignorance. "No child wishes to be born into turmoil. A birth is a time for joy. That way the child will not protest leaving its mother's body. If the mother focuses on the pain, it soon becomes unbearable."

Chenoa's simple reasoning sent relief straight through all three men. Lee considered his wife and the light dancing in her dark eyes. She enjoyed being needed. The way his society viewed her was very limited. The more time he spent with her the more he noticed his own ignorance. Chenoa lifted her eyes to smile at him as he considered her.

"I should stay with Nacoma tonight. She is very tired."

"But she's in no danger?"

That authority was edging her husband's voice. "She is strong but newborns can be restless. I will stay with her to tend to Tadi, so Nacoma can rest."

"Let me stay with her." Kiril felt like he would go insane if he couldn't at least lay his eyes on Nacoma. Just for a moment to see for himself. The waiting had been endless.

The junior officer aimed his serious eyes at her. Chenoa found herself softening toward him. Maybe he knew nothing about babies but with the way he looked at Nacoma...it was time he learned.

Chenoa nodded and Kiril was gone before she finished. He slipped through the door on silent feet, firmly shutting the door behind his body. A large hand gently settled around her neck. Chenoa sighed as Lee rubbed at her sore muscles.

"Nacoma is not the only one who needs some rest." Lee slid his hand down her back and gently pushed her forward. Warmth spread out from his touch in a wave of heat that settled into her body but also bled into her soul. She felt so complete right then, both in mind and spirit.

It was too bad there weren't more babies to deliver on the outpost. It was too bad the fence was being rebuilt.

It was simply too bad they could not live together. Chenoa signed again. She should not be so greedy. Most of her friends dreamed of having husbands. They went to their lonely beds with wool blankets instead of a man who made their blood rush. Life was not perfect.

Not in either world.

* * * * *

"Is their singing getting better or am I getting used to it?"

Kiril looked up and shrugged. Lee raised an eyebrow at the informal response but Kiril grinned instead. Little Tadi gurgled happily on the junior officer's lap as her mother tended the rapidly growing garden.

The Indian women certainly knew their art because what had once been a desolate spot of earth was now lush and green. Some of the plants were head high after a few short months. Chenoa had put Javier's wedding gift of seeds to good use. The fresh food the women produced was highly coveted on the compound.

The baby was coveted too. Nacoma often remarked that it was good she was the only one who could feed the infant. Otherwise she would never get to hold her own daughter. There were two older enforcers waiting behind Kiril right now to claim a moment with the baby should the officer give them the chance.

Lee tickled the baby's chin. She immediately wrapped her fingers around his large one. Pulling on his hand, Tadi tried to pop Lee's finger into her mouth.

"You're not shy. Are you, sweetheart?"

Kiril gently rocked the baby using his knee. "Princesses don't have to be shy."

"But they need to be shared." Xan flexed his fingers. "Give over, Kiril. You're hogging the baby again."

The women's singing stopped abruptly. Xan thrust Tadi back into Kiril's arms as he swung toward the garden at lightning speed. Brenda was crumpled among the plants, her face a pasty white.

Brenda lifted her eyes with total confusion. She didn't remember lying down. Her body felt horribly hot. Suddenly she felt her stomach knot with nausea and frantically tried to get to her feet. She didn't question how she'd gotten into her house.

Xan picked her hunched form up from the bathroom floor and she was simply too miserable to care. Her head was pounding. Xan smoothed her hair back from her face as he began examining her body.

"Brenda, you can't keep up with Chenoa."

She lifted her eyes to stare into Xan's frustrated face. His eyes were sympathetic as they brushed her face.

"Are you saying I'm too weak?" Her face burned with shame. Brenda touched her cheek and marveled at the fact that she could actually blush.

Pushing up from the bed, she brushed her husband's hands away. "Well, I'm just going to have to get stronger." Determination fired her but her head swam in a dizzy haze the second she stood up. Xan caught her and deposited her right back onto the bed again.

Tears flooded her eyes. Brenda felt the drops sliding down her cheeks and couldn't stop them. Xan looked at her in horrified confusion. She hadn't cried in front of someone in twenty years. But Brenda just couldn't seem to stop the flood of emotion.

Xan appeared with a wet towel, which she gratefully covered her eyes with. A deep cough escaped her next. Xan frowned deeply at his wife. It wasn't that he wanted to think of Brenda as weak but she simply didn't have the stamina Chenoa did.

Brenda coughed again, making him shake his head. She was sick. Eating all that fresh food had resulted in her immune system dropping. What bothered him was the fact that Brenda didn't look any less healthy. It was the honest truth that he sort of liked the new color of her skin.

Looking over her body with a practiced eye, Xan noticed the few pounds she'd gained. The weight did her good. Her breasts were round and plump. The soft globes of flesh looked absolutely mouthwatering on his willow-thin wife. For that matter, she'd grown some nice little curves on her hips and Xan fully approved. It couldn't be more than maybe five pounds but suddenly his wife just looked…healthy. A soft rap landed on the door. Chenoa stuck her head in a second later.

"I have brought Brenda some bread. It will settle her stomach."

"I'm not hungry." Brenda tried to stifle a sniffle as she pressed the towel tightly to her face.

"If you leave nothing in your stomach, the acid will only make it worse again." Nacoma plucked the towel away and smiled her over-large smile at Brenda's pouting lips. "Tomatoes are very acidic. They always made me sick in the beginning. You should not eat any more of them."

Chenoa and Nacoma simply took over. Xan watched as they lifted Brenda up by her arms and propped her back with pillows. Brenda didn't get the chance to protest as they fed her their bread. Chenoa even rinsed the towel out and returned to wipe the last few tears from Brenda's face.

"There. Do not be so worried. The emotions are very normal. Nacoma couldn't decide whether to laugh or cry half the time. It was always one or the other."

Their words didn't make a whole lot of sense to Xan but his wife's color suddenly bloomed. Her checks became rosy and her eyes sparkled. Even her lips grew ruby red as she let them curve into a slight smile. It would appear bread had more uses than Xan ever knew about.

Brenda chewed another mouthful of bread and couldn't help but sigh. It was amazing how much better she felt. In fact, she was almost jumping with energy. Chenoa reached out and laid a hand right on her belly. Brenda stared at the Indian woman with shock as Chenoa moved her fingers in a practiced manner.

"You are fortunate. Some woman have sickness much sooner."

His wife lost her color again and Xan was positive he lost his too. His eyes flew to Brenda's abdomen but he wasn't certain. Grabbing his medical bag he pulled a scan unit from it. Pressing the small terminal into Brenda's palm performed the most basic of blood analyses. It would give him her glucose level, her blood pressure and heart rate.

But the unit would also immediately test for pregnancy. Medical personnel were required to test for it immediately on any female being treated. If a woman was pregnant, she would receive the best treatment immediately. Absolutely no chance was taken with the life of an unborn baby.

Xan stared at the flashing screen in disbelief. He tossed it aside and grabbed his backup unit. Three seconds later it was flashing a positive warning at him.

"It just can't be." Brenda whispered her words as she stared at the flashing unit. Chenoa and Nacoma watched the couple with growing alarm. Xan's face suddenly turned into a furious mask. He flattened both his hands on either side of his wife.

"What did Javier buy for you to take?"

Brenda felt her heart stop. The last three months had been pure bliss. Xan had never once spoken about the past. He was deeply angry now. Her heart constricted as she considered losing him again. Brenda knew she'd never survive the loss.

"What drug did you take?"

"None." Xan's face became enraged but Brenda felt her own temper rising to meet him. She wouldn't lose him without a fight! "I haven't taken anything!"

"Damn it, Brenda! I won't have you risking prison!"

Brenda suddenly laughed. She was so happy! So wonderfully happy! Xan was worried she'd go to prison. He wanted her. Maybe even needed her. Slapping her hands over his stiff jaw, she planted a solid kiss onto his set lips.

"I love you too much to be so stupid again. I swear I didn't take anything." Brenda shook her head and laid both her hands over her belly. She laughed softly under her breath as her fingers gently found the enlarged shape of her growing womb. One of Xan's large hands joined hers as he searched her eyes.

"We both should have noticed...um...that I haven't had a period since moving in."

Chenoa pulled Nacoma along with her. The couple's words slipped into soft tones, which betrayed their deep affection. Chenoa felt her own eyes flood with tears. They were tears born of joy.

* * * * *

"Lee, that was an order." Russell's voice didn't sound very firm over the communications line. Lee's face never changed.

"Understood. Out." Punching the control to sever the link didn't bring Lee any measure of satisfaction. The order wasn't bugging him. It was the execution of it he would rather avoid.

It was time for Chenoa to testify. That wasn't unexpected. Russell was insisting she travel into the capital for the trial. Command was making the case a high profile one as an example to the general population.

Not an altogether bad idea. All except for the part about Chenoa taking part in the media feeding frenzy. Lee shoved his chair back in frustration. All right, he'd used the trial as an excuse to keep Chenoa manageable when she'd first arrived. That was the real problem. It was just twisting his gut to think she'd be disappointed in him.

Despite the early afternoon hour, Lee headed straight for his transport. He'd been completely aware of his actions at the time. Chenoa would have to understand he'd gained a better view of her since then.

His gut twisted tighter. There would be dozens of powerful men clamoring for her attention. The idea made him furious. Raising his hand, Lee turned the driver around.

The first thing he needed to do was buy his wife a wedding ring. Something huge that he wouldn't let her set foot off the compound without.

And than he'd make certain she never even thought about leaving him. Deception or not, she was his wife.

* * * * *

Chenoa detested her promise. The words were haunting her. She did not want to go to...that...greed-poisoned place!

But the truth was, she didn't want her husband to go there either. The women in his world were forward and brazen. They were like jackals that might steal her husband from her. Brenda's words had cut a deep track across her heart.

Divorce.

A single word that could cause so very much pain. She ached just thinking about it. Raising her eyes she considered her husband. Strength still rose from him like light. She felt a quiver inside her belly as she watched his eyes turn into a raptor's gaze.

Woman would covet him. Here on the compound there was peace. Chenoa had immersed herself in it to avoid remembering the harsh truth about Lee's world.

He held the right to set her aside.

Lee couldn't stand it. Chenoa's eyes were full of pain. It tore his heart out. But he wouldn't let her go, not now or ever. Reaching for her, Lee pulled her body to his with all of the frustration they seemed surrounded by. This had been how they'd always communicated best. Body to body. Explanations and motivations didn't mean a thing. It became male and female uniting in a bond as old as time.

"Yes. I want you to touch me." Chenoa let her head fall back as her husband smoothed his large hands over her. Maybe desperation was driving her but it mixed with arousal in a potent elixir that numbed her wounds. Chenoa wanted to become intoxicated.

"Then bare your breasts for me."

She liked the arrogance in his voice tonight. Flicking the button open, Chenoa watched his eyes devour each tiny amount of skin she revealed to him. She felt her breath catch as power engulfed her. His raptor's eyes were like slaves to her. Another button released and the dress slipped down to catch on her nipples. They were hard little points that snagged the material, preventing the last delicate part of her from being seen.

"All of them. Show me your nipples."

"No." His eyes flashed as Chenoa gently fingered her nipples through the dress. "I want you to bare your body for me first."

Her husband obeyed. Chenoa felt her breasts lift with arousal as she looked at his body. His strength still made her feel small. He was a man who held control tightly in his fist. Otherwise he would have hurt her. But she had never feared him. This man had honor.

Chenoa laughed when his hands closed onto her waist. Lifting her high he spun them both around 'til her dress went slithering down her body. The garment whipped across the room and hit the wall.

Lee felt his staff harden painfully as her sex became even with his face. He could smell her heat. Smell the moist scent of her folds. "Wrap your legs around me." Her thighs gripped his waist as Lee lowered her until his staff was probing her passage.

His hands settled onto her bottom, firmly gripping each cheek as Lee lowered her onto his sex. He pulled her up and lowered her again.

"More." She moaned the demand. Desire was pounding through his body as Lee held complete control of their coupling. Lowing her body he let her passage glide down his length. She gasped with pleasure when he lifted her again. Her nipples stabbed into his chest as he impaled her and again when he lifted her.

Chenoa felt his need to master. She surrendered to it gracefully. Her body was one complete point of sensation. His body triggered the pulses that sent her blood rushing along her veins. She moaned as he lifted her and gasped when he denied her climax.

"Look at me." His voice was harsh with need. Chenoa lifted her eyes to find his glowing in primal glory. "Let me watch your pleasure."

Lee dropped her onto the hard thrust of his body and she moaned. Her eyes became liquid pools as her passage suddenly gripped his sex, pulling and clutching around him. He erupted into her body while she stared into his eyes.

Lee didn't let her feet touch the floor. He enjoyed laying her in his bed. Following her down onto the soft surface, he pulled a tight nipple into his mouth. He was still hard with need. Desire pounded against his temples as the scent of warm skin filled his nostrils.

His sex pulsed against her hip, making Chenoa purr. Heat traveled her body in lazy waves that centered under his mouth as it suckled from her breast. She spread her body wide for him, wanting to end any distance between them. The smooth glide of his body into hers made her purr yet again. Raising her hips, she matched the rhythm she knew would bring them both satisfaction.

Urgency wasn't overwhelming this time. Lee groaned as pure enjoyment coursed through his body. Her passage was slick and tight. He rode her with deep thrusts that made her moan, the deep husky hum making his blood pound even faster. It was a pure, honest sound, not one she'd practiced to stroke his ego. Her hands scratched at his arms making little marks that he'd carry tomorrow. Lee pressed his body deeper into hers in response. The walls of her passage began to twist around his staff like a vise, preparing to milk him once again when pleasure spiked through her. Her eyes flew open when the climax ripped along her body, her hips frantically pressed up, and Lee ground himself into her body with a savage growl to empty himself into her deepest core.

* * * * *

The trip to Lee's civilized world was a desolate one. Chenoa stared at the endless miles of barren land. Their transport moved forward for what seemed like hours. Her mouth was dry from looking at the miles of sand and scrub brush.

The city the desert gave way to wasn't much better. Chenoa watched the sand become endless black roads that twisted between ugly buildings. Hordes of people traveled the footpaths next to the buildings. They wore harsh faces that didn't lift with greeting to one another.

Lee grasped her hand, giving it a firm squeeze. His golden-brown eyes were etched with tight concern as they continued their never-ending scrutiny of the world outside the transport's windows. "We'll clear the projects soon."

"What are projects?" Her husband's eyes made another survey of their surroundings before retuning to her face.

"This is the most run-down part of the city. Fifty years ago it was a thriving area. Now, it's where the poorest people live."

"They look so tired." But the buildings began to change. Instead of dirty footpaths, there were shimmering white stones to walk on. Lush flowering plants were displayed in colorful stone boxes. The buildings rose into the sky with gleaming sides that held sparkling windows.

Small transports jammed the streets as they drew in close to a huge sparkling structure of glass. Its domed top rose up into the afternoon sun. Sitting in front of it was a huge fountain that sprayed streams of crystal clear water in different directions.

But no one was playing in the water. Chenoa remembered the way Nacoma's nieces had frolicked in the market fountain. This was a magnificent display yet it was oddly empty. The people passing by didn't even look at its sparkling beauty. They held tiny communication devices to their ears and spoke into them as their feet hurried forward.

The transport turned a corner and skidded to an abrupt halt. Chenoa pitched forward. Her husband sent out a solid arm to hold her steady. Light suddenly illuminated the transport in blinding amounts. The windows of the transport were covered by lights and hands that frantically tapped for attention.

"Get us through those gates."

Lee barked his command as his arm pressed Chenoa back into the seat. The media swarmed around them like insects. The enforcer next to her sat forward and placed his shoulders in front of the transports window. Lee did the same. Chenoa listened to the tapping become even more frenzied as the driver inched their transport forward.

Suddenly, it was all gone. The driver wiped his forearm across his forehead as he moved the vehicle forward. Lee aimed his hawk's eyes at her face, intently studying her reaction.

"What was that?" Her husband's face became guarded as he rubbed his hand across her cheek. The caress reminded Chenoa of a farewell kiss. A fine tremor of foreboding shook her body.

The transport suddenly stopped. The door was pulled open in the very same instant.

"Commander Tanner, welcome to Salsona." Her husband took his time exiting the transport. Chenoa knew his body's movement well. It was as if he lingered in the doorway to shield her from whoever was greeting him. He turned his huge frame and offered a hand toward her.

Laying her hand in his made her heart race with apprehension. Chenoa stepped into the afternoon sunlight and blinked. There were endless numbers of people crowded together waiting for her. They held themselves in an odd hushed silence that let her ears catch their gasps the second she appeared. Huge smiles were plastered to their faces and aimed directly at her.

"You must be Chenoa." Her host tried to capture her hand but Lee settled it onto his arm instead. Chenoa watched the man's eyes flicker with annoyance before he brightened his smile yet again.

"I'm Cameron Russell. Welcome."

Chenoa felt anything but welcome! She felt like a prize heifer being presented at the monthly livestock auction back on her Peoples' land. Raising her chin, she pressed her lips into a firm line. The crowd pressed in on them making her shift closer to Lee's huge body.

Cameron Russell began what was an endless amount of introductions. Every person who stepped up to meet her had titles attached to their name. It became a tangled mess inside her head before even half of the assembled group had shaken her hand.

The afternoon sun beat down on her head making tiny drops of perspiration dampen her hair. Sweat was beaded across many of the men who continued to step forward to get their introduction. Still, Cameron Russell carried on with the names and titles and ranks.

Chenoa suddenly lifted her eyes to search the crowd. There wasn't a single woman there. Desperation began pulsing through her brain as she watched the sea of eyes inspect every inch of her body. Seconds evolved into hours under the tight scrutiny.

"Would you care to settle into your rooms, my dear?"

Chenoa frowned with the use of the familiar endearment. She'd come to consider the word something intimate between Lee and herself. It sounded far too forward coming from a stranger.

"Yes sir, we would." Her husband pulled her halfway behind his frame as he faced off with their host. Cameron's face drew tight with anger as Lee refused to let the man touch her again.

"Well yes, right this way, please."

The huge domed building was shimmering white inside. The sunbeams shattered as they came through the glass dome. The room was filled with gleaming beams of light. Green plants grew inside the building and water bubbled up through small fountains. Every surface shone from recent polishing.

"Here we are. I hope you don't mind but my sister took the liberty of selecting a dress for you to wear tonight. Just a welcome gathering, nothing too grand."

"Commander Tanner, you are expected in the briefing chamber."

"Yes, sir." Lee growled the words as Russell smirked at him. He considered the room and nodded.

"You must go?" Chenoa didn't like the wave of weakness she felt in response to the idea of her husband departing.

"They won't bother you in here. Just keep the door locked." Lee stroked her cheek before cupping her chin and finding her lips. His communication unit buzzed for attention making him growl. Russell had a hell of a lot of nerve.

"Do you remember how to use the communication panel?"

"Yes." Chenoa forced her back straight. She was clinging to him like a child to its mother. She gave him a smile as she laced her fingers tightly together to hide their trembling. "You need not worry about me, Husband."

That was open to debate! Lee hid his frustration as his wife stepped away from him. "Try and nap. Tonight might run late."

The door slid shut leaving her with her thoughts. Chenoa pushed the lock button before turning to consider her surroundings.

The door of the room was doublewide and both were open to display a room that was bigger than her grandmother's entire house.

She suddenly felt so very alone. Her eyes traveled the room in all its hugeness. Some might call it grand. Maybe she was ignorant to consider it lacking but this wasn't a home. Lee's officer housing was far more inviting.

Besides, what a waste of space! Was there not some cause in this world that could use the money that had built this palace? A garden would have better served these people. That would have shared the wealth instead of hoarding it for but a few members of the tribe.

She knew it wasn't her place to judge others but Chenoa simply couldn't help it. The things truly worth having in life were not the items that you could hold in your hands. Instead it was the love that filled your heart that made you rich with spirit.

Chenoa felt the corners of her lips sink down. Lee had seemed so very formal. He had never treated her with such…detachment before. The fear she'd tried to bury rose up in her heart as she considered his impersonal attitude.

Divorce. A single word that would shatter her heart. Chenoa knew such a blow would certainly kill her. Fat tears welled in her eyes. Running a soft hand over her belly, she tried to gently rub her growing babe.

The tears dropped down her cheeks as her emotions surged forward like an afternoon thunderstorm. Her pregnancy was new but it seemed that she wasn't any more immune to the hormones than Brenda had been. But her body hid the two-month-old baby much better than Brenda's thin frame. Lee hadn't even noticed yet. That made even more tears drop from her eyes. The man knew her body intimately but he hadn't noticed such a change.

Wiping at her face, Chenoa found a small sofa in the corner of the room. She dropped into it and closed her eyes. She couldn't sleep in the bed. It was simply too huge. The back of the sofa rose up to support her back and she let herself drift off into slumber.

She should not have taken the nap. Chenoa forced her lips into a pleasant line while she ground her teeth together. No, she never should have slept. Now her mind was far too alert. She'd rather drift through this party with a brain that was too tired to absorb details.

Instead she was keenly aware of each and every second. Well, at least there was food that didn't stink. Chenoa looked at one of the long, fabric-draped tables and felt her mouth water. There were trays of ripe strawberries and purple boysenberries. They were shiny from water making them look even better.

Most of the food she didn't recognize but those fresh berries were calling to her. The group of men surrounding her didn't seem to notice her eyes fixed on the table. Instead they clamored for her attention.

Chenoa jerked her eyes back to the horde clustered around her. She needed to watch them carefully. They seemed to think she was some kind of exotic pet. Right in the middle of conversation they would reach for her and pet her. An arm, her back, her hair, any part of her body they could reach. The dress she was wearing didn't help either.

The fabric was beautiful but as soft as warm butter. It lay over her body, exposing her every curve. There was a deep V cut at the neck that gave a view of her breasts to anyone standing in front of her. The skirt fell to her toes, yet it was tight and that forced her to walk with small steps.

"Ah, my dear. You are truly radiant." Russell glided up to claim a spot in front of her. The man's face was wearing a smug grin as he inspected her body from head to toe. Chenoa ground her teeth tighter. Russell's eyes lingered over her belly. His hand actually lifted toward her.

"Where is Lee?"

Russel frowned darkly at her. "He's a busy man, my dear."

The man tried to catch her hand again. She stepped on the bottom of her dress as she jumped away from him.

Grabbing a handful of her skirt, Chenoa pulled the fabric away from her ankles as she turned and left. Let them think her rude, she didn't care! But every direction she looked held groups of more men with over bright smiles.

"Chenoa, would you join a friend for some refreshments?" Javier surfaced from the crowd and offered his arm. Men who were quickly closing in on her suddenly stopped in their tracks at the appearance of Javier.

"You cannot imagine how much I would like to share your company."

The man chuckled deeply as Chenoa curled her fingers around his arm. He spared her a small grin before he raised his head to scowl at the men closest to them. They fell back like a pack of scavengers that recognized a more dominant predator.

Chenoa couldn't control the low hiss that came out of her throat. Javier raised an eyebrow as he steered her toward the strawberries. "I quite agree with you."

"How can you? This is your world." Her stomach rumbled as she caught the scent of food. Nausea was keeping her company 'til noon each day. But by nightfall she was starving. The fruit was too big a temptation.

"I'm not so sure about that." Javier lifted a small plate and handed it to her. The man looked over the crowd with a discontentment that made his eyes flare open. But she looked past the man, dropping her plate onto the marble floor. It shattered into pieces.

"What is she doing to my husband?" It was a stupid question. Chenoa knew what kissing looked like! A silver-haired woman was wrapped around Lee as she pressed her lips to his.

The room had gone silent the second she dropped the plate. Chenoa's outraged question bounced off the walls, reaching every single man's ears. It also reached the woman kissing Lee.

The silver-blonde sprang away from Lee as the room erupted into furious outbursts.

"Husband!"

"Who the hell married her?"

"Like hell she's married!"

Javier tipped his head back and laughed. His huge body shook with his amusement. The guests converged on Russell, as they demanded to know if she was married. The silver-blonde scurried out of the room as Chenoa propped her hands onto her hips and glared at her husband. She might be a savage but no woman would take her place so easily.

Lee aimed his glowing hawk's eyes at her. He strode across the room on determined feet. A small grin turned up the corners of his mouth making her hiss with frustration. Lee hooked her waist with his arm and yanked her against his body despite her outrage.

"Good evening, Mrs. Tanner." She wriggled in his embrace but he held her firmly in place as his lips branded her. It was an arrogant display of physical superiority. But Chenoa felt her breasts lift against the solid strength of his chest, her nipples drawing into tight buttons that stabbed forward in invitation. Lee lifted his head and grunted with approval. Her cheeks were flushed and her lips lightly swollen. He turned her to face the room. It was a primitive method of making certain every last man in the place knew exactly who Chenoa belonged to.

Lee was convinced he was going to kill that next man who even tried to touch his woman. Russell was damn lucky his sister had stopped Lee from charging across the room.

Chenoa stomped on his foot again. He raised an eyebrow at her before wrapping one huge hand completely around her wrist. "Excuse us, gentlemen. My wife is tired. Good night."

Lee strode from the room with Chenoa forced to keep pace with him. Her fury bubbled over her manners the second they cleared the large ornate doors that admitted them both to her room. "Let me go!"

"No." His voice was whisper-soft. A flick of his wrist pulled her body into his embrace as Lee tipped her head back so his eyes could probe into hers. "Lydia kissed me."

"This I saw with my own eyes." Chenoa shrank against his body but she was held secure as his eyes began to glow like a raptor preparing to hunt. One solid arm clamped around her waist and lifted her feet from the floor. Chenoa froze as she clung to him out of instinct.

His eyes lit with arrogant pleasure. "The women of my world aren't as controlled with their bodies."

Chenoa felt her blood drain from her face. Her deepest fear of coming to the city had been that her husband would find it far too easy to set her aside.

"But I did not kiss her back."

He growled at her beneath his breath. Chenoa felt the color return to her cheeks in a rush that left her dizzy. He was furious with her for doubting him. His eyes turned to pure gold as he considered the task of proving to her his determination to be her mate.

Desperation erupted inside her as she watched his eyes drop to her mouth. "Yes." Chenoa ground her lips into his as she tried to erase every last trace of the silver-blonde woman. This was her mate! She would remind him why she was the only woman he would ever need.

His mouth was arrogant. His tongue thrust into her mouth and Chenoa sent her own to stab back at his. They dueled in a mimicry of the motion their bodies would succumb to when they joined together in intimacy.

Tearing her lips away from his, Chenoa felt her own little growl rumble from her chest. The predator inside her husband was free. It stared at her with glowing eyes that demanded her compliance. "I loathe this dress. Strip it from me, Husband."

Amusement lit his face as he lowered her to the floor. "Yes, ma'am." The fabric split with a sharp sound as Lee used his large hands to tear it straight down its front. Chenoa smiled as it became a useless pile of cloth. Never would she be displayed so again.

She sighed as the night air drifted over her skin. She was deliciously free and bare. Chenoa looked at her mate and frowned. "Take your clothes off." He raised another dark eyebrow in the face of her order. Chenoa tossed her head in challenge.

"Yes, ma'am." She smiled a very naughty smile as Lee reached for his uniform's fashioning. His wife was enjoying her moment of control. So was he. Dropping his pants aside he slowly ran a sure hand over his hard weapon. Her eyes followed the motion as Lee stroked it again. "I approve of your possessiveness, Chenoa." He released his weapon and it rose straight up from his body with stiff promise.

"Take me back to the desert." Chenoa's words echoed his own desires. Lee hooked an arm around her waist to pull her next to him. Their naked flesh clashed like thunder clouds setting off bolts of desire that stabbed both of them with brilliant intensity.

"Wrap your legs around me." His words were low. Chenoa shivered as she felt the hard thrust of his sex against her belly. As she lifted her thighs, the hard length of his rod dropped free to thrust against the deepest folds of her body. She was moist and swollen for him. The scent of her own arousal drifted up to her, making desire twist even tighter inside her passage. The hard staff of his erection brushed against her spread sex making her moan.

Lee grasped one cheek of her bottom in each of his hands. His staff was slick from the welcoming flow coming from her body. Lifting her bottom, he lowered her back onto his length. Tight and hot, her body gripped his length, making sweat bead on his forehead. But Lee wasn't going to come yet. He wanted to ride her and listen to her scream with pleasure. The pleasure only he could give her.

His hips hammered into her body but it wasn't fast. Instead Lee used his iron control to ride her with deep thrusts that buried his weapon in her to the hilt before he lifted her off his flesh again. Chenoa flung her head back as she arched her hips forward to sheathe his erection. Her hands clung to his powerful shoulders as pleasure began to twist into a hard knot of tension deep inside her belly. Everything centered on the thrust of his body. Each breath she drew was to continue the motion of her hips toward the driving force of his body.

"Look at me!" Lee demanded and Chenoa willingly obeyed him. His eyes glowed with triumph as she lifted her eyelids to let him probe her thoughts. "Now find your pleasure."

Lee watched her eyes turn to liquid. He quickened his pace and felt her passage clench around his staff. But she never closed her eyes. Instead she let him watch the wave of sensation crest inside her as her lips released a moan of pure delight.

Chenoa smiled at her husband. He liked to watch her. In fact she sensed he needed to watch her climax. It was part of some dominating male instinct. She was still impaled on his staff. His erection as stiff and hard as the moment she'd clasped her thighs around him. "You enjoy doing that to me."

"I do."

Her voice was husky and naughty. Lee let his lips tug into a grin. He enjoyed it with a furious need. He'd never felt emotion attached to his sexual needs before. He turned and walked toward the bed. The movements sent his staff into Chenoa with quick jerks that made Lee tighten his jaw. The need to release his seed into her body became pressing. The walls of her passage had tightened with her climax making it torture to delay his own pleasure.

"Umm...yes, Husband! More! Give me all of you!" Lee sprawled himself over her willing body and rode her with hard thrusts. Chenoa abandoned herself to him completely. Lee sunk into the depths of intimacy as his body pounded into her flesh with driving need.

Chenoa felt her body tighten again as her husband's staff erupted inside her. His groan split the quiet room as she moaned with him. They weren't separate beings. Instead they were bound together in the spirit as tightly as their flesh merged.

Lee rolled off her body and pulled her along 'til her head lay pillowed on his chest. Chenoa listened to the sound of his heart as it drove life through his body. She laid a hand over her flat belly and smiled with maternal knowledge. She understood now. Her grandmother's wisdom floated across her memory as she considered the child she would share with Lee.

A large hand stroked her face and tipped it up to meet her husband's golden eyes. He considered the smile resting on her face. Chenoa reached for his hand and laid it across her belly but no hint of understanding crossed his face.

"Our child is growing."

Chapter Thirteen

"They are completely unreasonable."

"Of course, they're men. It is most cruel that they are so limited." Nacoma smiled and Chenoa ground her teeth together. Brenda pushed her lips out into a pout. Nacoma's smile turned into an expression of horror as she considered the garden. Lee and Xan were busy directing the tending of it.

Nacoma flew away from the two mothers-to-be with her arms waving in the air. Chenoa considered her husband as he yanked a young corn stalk out of the ground. Nacoma grabbed the plant and scolded the commander with fierce words.

Chenoa stood up and went back into her house. "Come on, Brenda. I refuse to sit here with the day so young." The small house was a welcome sight to her eyes. Chenoa smiled as she looked over the tiny three-roomed structure.

She would more gladly lay her head here than in any palace! A tiny frown marred her face but Chenoa wiped it away. Her husband was furious with her. Yet she wasn't sorry. The only thing she regretted was not telling him about the pregnancy in time to save herself that trip into the city.

Lee would adjust in time. She didn't care about anyone else. Let them be angry that she was married. Her pregnancy had gotten her shipped back to the outpost before dawn.

That pleased Chenoa quite nicely!

"Chenoa." Her husband's voice was a soft growl. A large hand curled around her belly as he nuzzled her neck. "You will rest."

"Have you seen Tadi?"

Lee felt his forehead crease. His wife was going to apply some of that logic of hers again. "Yes."

"Why then do you doubt that I know what is healthy for this time in my life?" Chenoa turned in Lee's embrace. "Yet I would have told you sooner if I had known I could stay home."

Lee didn't like the trace of fear that flashed through his memory in response. He'd never even considered Chenoa might be pregnant. Hell, the truth was he'd never even dreamed of having his own child. The odds against it were too high to calculate. Hearing that *his child* was growing inside her body while they were in a city that hadn't seen a single human birth in two decades sent his heart into his throat.

He still couldn't leave her for an entire day. Russell and his list of people could go straight to hell. Chenoa dropped her hand and rubbed his sex through his uniform. Lee snatched her wrist and raised it to his lips. She frowned deeply at him.

"The doctors forbid any sex." It was a fact Lee didn't care for. His staff had risen firmly in response to her touch. The warm scent of her skin made him harden even more.

"Xan and Brenda have been as man and wife and her child pushes her belly forward."

Lee raised an eyebrow. "Really?" Chenoa raised her opposite hand to resume stroking his hard sex. She purred deeply as she rubbed her breasts against his chest. "Brenda says her nipples are very sensitive now. Just a moment of sucking makes her beg to be ridden." His hips thrust forward into her hand as he groaned deeply. Chenoa lifted her eyelids to see his eyes begin to glow.

"Excuse me, sir." Xan stood in the doorway admiring the table in order to keep his eyes off Chenoa. Lee turned toward his officer. He firmly set his jaw against the confinement of his uniform over the swollen bulge of his staff. Xan raised his eyes with a solemn face. "We've got company."

Chenoa followed her husband to look out into the front drive. One of the transports was pulled up in the outer compound. Two women stood there with a mountain of luggage piled next to them in the dirt. They turned toward her husband and waved.

"Hello, Lee! We're here!"

Chenoa felt her stomach drop clean to her toes. The same silver-blonde from the city picked up her feet and ran toward her husband. The woman flung her body into Lee's arms while she hugged him. Her entire body wiggled against her husband's huge frame.

Fat tears welled up in her eyes. Chenoa wiped them away with an angry swipe of her hand. She would not cry in defeat! Instead, Chenoa lifted her chin and walked down the steps toward their...guests.

The blonde's eyes caught her as she approached. A bright smile appeared on the woman's face as she looked at Chenoa.

Suddenly, the blonde let Lee go and dashed around her husband's body as she charged toward Chenoa. The girl stopped just a mere foot in front of her as her face became split with a huge smile. Her blue eyes sparkled with unshed tears.

"I'm so happy to be here! You left so quickly that we didn't get to meet but I'm so happy to be here!"

The woman's words all ran together. Chenoa didn't think she even knew what was coming out of her mouth. The brilliance of her smile simply confounded her. Were the women from Lee's world happy about sharing their men? Was Chenoa expected to welcome her as a sister?

"Chenoa?" Lee stepped between the blonde and her as she raised her smoldering eyes to him. "This is Lydia. She wanted —"

"This is my friend, Freya!" Lydia yanked the other woman in front of Chenoa and pushed Lee aside. Freya immediately plastered a smile onto her face that didn't quite reach her hazel eyes. Instead Chenoa noticed the deep fear lurking there.

Lee set his jaw before he tried to finish the introductions. "Lydia and Freya want to learn how to plant a garden."

"Oh yes! I've heard so much about this one. It's the biggest one on the continent that isn't behind a reservation wall. We can't wait to begin! We want to know everything!"

Her husband sounded unimpressed with the women's reasoning. Chenoa pressed her lips into a firm line as well. She could not outright accuse them of lying but their words sounded hollow.

So, she would teach them how to garden.

But tonight, she would teach her husband that he didn't have enough strength for more than one wife.

Chenoa's lips lifted into a grin as she considered her husband's powerful shoulders. Yes, tonight she would be the one in control.

* * * * *

Desert sand was almost impossible to wash out of hair. Lee hit the control on his shower and turned it up to its full pressure. He had no idea how his wife kept her mane of hair clean.

"Mmmm...I think you need some help." Lee jerked his eyes open as Chenoa stepped into the shower. Brilliantly nude, she lifted her head toward the water spray and purred as it slid down her neck. His sex sprang to instant attention. Her slim hand curled around the hard flesh making him groan. But she was in front of the shower door and Lee couldn't exactly shove her out of the way.

"Chenoa... No sex... That's going to kill me."

"Humm?" A low laugh hit his ears as her fingers found the spot at the top of his staff that made his body jerk. "I think you will live."

Her warm skin filled his senses. Lee growled again as he watched her drop down his body to her knees. Threading his fingers through the wet strands of her hair he watched her take his sex into her mouth. "To hell with the doctor."

She purred again as her tongue flicked over his sex. Lee thrust forward toward the delicious torment as she took more of him into her hot mouth. She sucked and pulled on his sex making his teeth clench. Climax was maddeningly close. Spikes of sensation ripped through his staff as her tongue flicked up and down its length.

Chenoa drew his stiff erection into her mouth again. Her husband's groan fed her boldness. She was addicted to his body but also to the power of making him respond. Licking his staff, she pressed her hands to his rigid thighs, purring with satisfaction over the thick muscles. His fingers gripped her head pressing her forward to ease his needs.

He took control from her, thrusting his body into hers with tight jerks. His staff jumped in her mouth as it quivered to announce an approaching climax. Chenoa circled the hard flesh with her tongue, sucking it deeply into her throat. His seed erupted in a wide spray, which she let coat her mouth.

But she wasn't stopping. Chenoa licked his staff with long strokes. His sex never softened, instead it remained swollen with need.

Lee pulled her off her knees. Her lips were puffy from her efforts, making him groan softly in response. Need was coursing through him. Heat bled across his skin, making him more aware of her body — the hot smell of her arousal, the tight pucker of her nipples, the way her breasts were swollen with desire.

Her nipples were a darker hue. Lifting her up, Lee let the tempting globes hang in front of his face. He nuzzled against them, inhaling the smell of her skin before turning his lips to pull one of the sweet tips into his mouth.

"Yesss…" Chenoa wrapped her legs around her husband as he leaned her back against the shower wall. Steam rose in thick clouds around them making it impossibly hot. His mouth was liquid fire as it surrounded her nipple. Molten lava flowed in a deep river from her breast to her passage. The folds of her sex opened as her own moisture flowed from her center.

Lee sucked her breast into his mouth and licked the nipple. Chenoa gasped as a wave of pleasure swept her into a sea of painful arousal. Her passage ached to be filled. Her fingers curled into talons on his shoulders as the sensation rose to a fever pitch. Chenoa heard her heartbeat pounding in her ears. She thrust her hips toward her husband, begging for his flesh. The tip of his staff sank into her body, making her cry out with need. Lee's huge hands gripped her bottom as he used his strength to control her body, moving it to encase his length.

"You'll stay in bed tomorrow. All day long. I'm going to ride you 'til you can't stand up."

Chenoa lifted her eyelids to stare into the glowing eyes of her husband. There was a promise burning in his golden eyes that made her lick her lips. His hips drove into her. His flesh was even hotter than the steam that bathed their bodies. The harsh sound of his breath hit her ears as she felt her passage grip his staff.

Pleasure ripped through her body in an explosion that left her sagging against her husband's body. Lee laid small kisses along her neck as his chest rose with deep movements. It was a perfect moment of trust. Together they were merged into the most peaceful of unions. It was stunning because it was so very simple. Society wanted to warp the relationship, give it borders with rules.

None of it mattered. Only Lee and the way his body answered the yearnings of hers. It was simple…complete. "I love you." At her words, Lee's raptor eyes flew open to burn into hers. Chenoa smoothed her fingers over the frown his mouth set into. "And I expect you to keep your promise." Unwrapping her legs, Chenoa stepped out of the shower. She flung a look back at her husband. "I can walk quite well…Husband. If that is all you have, I will be up with the sun."

The naughty little challenge made Lee smile. He watched the way she moved across the bathroom with pure enjoyment. She was an amazing creature. Flowing satin and curves that drew his eyes to every last part of her body. A smile sat on her face as she raised an eyebrow in challenge.

Lee spread his arms out wide before giving her a deep growl. She laughed before turning on her heel to flee. He caught her before she cleared the bathroom door, tossing her squirming body into the air.

"I always keep my promises!" Strong arms clasped her to his chest as his feet carried them toward their dark bedroom. "Always!"

Chenoa was grateful for the night. Darkness shielded her from her husband's sharp eyes. Fear crept into her heart as she considered his words. Could he really be a man who walked a different path than most of his people? Would he honor his marriage vows when he had been raised by a people who seemed to discard such bonds whenever it suited them?

She could ask him. Lee was not a man who would not answer her. Yet Chenoa felt his hands begin to move over her body and she simply didn't want to know. Tonight she had her husband. If someday he would leave her, she intended to live today in ignorant bliss.

* * * * *

"They are hopeless." Nacoma tossed her thick braid of hair over her shoulder with an angry jerk of her head. Lydia and Freya were driving them both insane.

"They hate the dirt. They detest the sun," Nacoma continued mumbling about the two women.

"Yet they persist in coming out each morning. One cannot fault their willpower." Chenoa didn't understand it. The two modern women followed her around like puppies. The strong sun turned their fair skin red but they came out anyway. They wrinkled their noses as they ate the garden's fruits and asked for more.

Yet always the words that fell from their lips weren't what Chenoa saw written in their eyes. Frustration ate away at her a little more each night. Why were they there?

Chenoa shifted her eyes to consider the compound. It was different this morning. She could feel the tension rising off the men for some reason. Her eyes searched the familiar duty station yet found nothing of any great difference from yesterday.

A large column of transports was raising a cloud of dust as it approached the housing compound. Chenoa had learned to keep every window in her small house tightly closed against the dirt those transports threw into the air. Washing the outside of the window was a complete waste of time. Her grandmother would frown over the thick dirt sitting on the windowsills.

But the garden would please her. Chenoa smiled as she felt a tiny kick inside her belly. Her eyes grew misty as she rubbed her growing tummy. She was so close to her grandmother and still an eternity apart from her.

"Robert!" Lydia ran out of the garden in sheer joy. The woman raced toward the newly arrived transports and flung herself into a man's arms. He laughed deeply as he tossed her into the air before capturing her in a hug. Another man descended from the transport and held his arms open for Freya.

Kiril stood at attention next to their two visitors, his body clearly rigid. Whoever their visitors were, they must be important.

Chenoa watched as the two couples immediately left Kiril. They didn't spare the officer a single thought as they hurried toward the long row of housing units. Kiril shook his head at the abrupt behavior before he relaxed and walked toward the garden. Chenoa smiled as she watched the man find a reason to move closer to Nacoma. Her friend wasn't unkind to the junior officer but she never gave him any encouragement. She turned away after exchanging polite words with the man. Frustration crossed Kiril's face as he stared at the back of Nacoma's head.

Chenoa turned to consider the desert. She didn't want to intrude on the couple in the garden. Kiril needed all the help he might get with her stubborn friend but it was too early to take to the house. Moving over the golden sand she walked along a familiar trail. Half a mile later she stood looking over the construction of the new section of the fence. Security was tight here. Men stood with their eyes moving constantly over the surrounding dunes. They clutched their weapons like lifelines.

Very soon the fence would once again be completed. Chenoa looked onto the Peoples' land with hungry eyes. The men on duty were used to her standing there. As many times as she told herself to stop asking for more, she still did. She wanted her grandmother too.

But now she needed her grandmother as well. The idea of birthing her child without of her own people terrified her. She didn't trust the white man's doctors. Lee brought home his doctor's orders and Chenoa couldn't keep her laughter from spilling out of her mouth. Brenda would need help when it came time for her birthing.

No sex. Why ever not? How did they think the baby got into her womb in the first place? They wanted her to lay in bed. Ha! That would let her body become too weak to birth the baby. She was never to touch the home grown food from their garden. Instead Lee brought her food that was sealed inside of plastic that smelt rotten.

They knew so little! Nature simply needed to take its course. The garden grew under the summer sun and her child grew with the nourishment the garden yielded. Why did they not understand the earth's harmony?

Why couldn't she understand her husband? Love sprang up inside her heart so deep she couldn't escape it. The words had spilled out of her mouth because she was so full of the emotions. But Lee had said nothing in return.

How could he not love her? Was it even possible for one to be so full of love and not have it returned? If fate truly was so cruel, Chenoa didn't want to know.

"What is that?"

"Beats me."

The guards' eyes were drawn to the sand as they shifted from their duty stations to consider an animal. Chenoa laughed slightly as she eyed the bird. The rooster didn't give the men he passed any attention. Instead he walked by with an arrogant jerk of his head.

The bird walked right up to her feet. He raised his wings to beat at the air as he screeched out a warning. Chenoa bent to pick up the feisty bird. Life always found a way. The rooster had smelled her hens on the breeze and walked right off the Peoples' land to find the hens on the enforcers' compound.

Yes, nature was making sure the hens would be hatching up a nest full of chicks. Just as it had ensured that her own body would ripen with the season.

But would life ensure that her soul would be united in love? Chenoa shook her head. She would have to find the courage to ask her husband. Uncertainty nibbled at her will as she walked back toward her home. There was stability in leaving matters as they were.

But that wouldn't bring her the peace she kept reaching for. Maybe life was simply a cycle of uncertainty. Chenoa felt her face fall into a deep frown. Her grandmother had never taught her that life was so heavy to bear. Had she truly been so sheltered? To accept that, she would also be accepting that uncertainty would always walk beside her. Her heart rejected that burden. Love filled her heart when just months ago it had seemed impossible.

Turning back around, Chenoa looked at the blue glow of the fence. She had overcome that barrier once. She would do it again, because her grandmother was going to hold her great-grandchild.

That was a promise Chenoa intended to keep.

* * * * *

"It's simple enough to understand, Commander."

Lee curled his fingers into a fist. Robert Welsmon was a civilian. That was the only reason Lee wasn't going to smash his jaw into pieces. The fact that the man was on the ruling planetary council didn't mean a thing, compared to what he was trying to force down Lee's throat.

"Good. I knew you'd see the logic. After that display at the reception, Councilman Trouse felt you'd be resistant to the idea. Thank you for not being difficult."

The man walked away. Lee considered the man's back with anger burning along every inch of his body. He would never give Chenoa up. Not to her fears and certainly not to a bunch of greedy men who thought their money made their demands worth listening to.

"Sir?" The title made Lee's temper boil. Out here there were men who believed in the enforcer codes. How in the hell had men made it onto the council who didn't know a thing about honor? "Yes, Lieutenant?"

"If you are going to post a resignation, I'd like to join you."

Xan's blue eyes were harsh as he stared into Lee's. Councilman Welsmon hadn't even kept his voice low enough to contain the words. Xan's face was etched with fury.

"I haven't made any decisions." Lee's words were sharp. Most men would have left after hearing them. Xan's eyes narrowed but the man stood firmly in his tracks.

"As I told you before, Lieutenant, I'm handling the situation."

And that was exactly what Lee intended to do. No one was going to touch his wife!

* * * * *

Chenoa propped her hands onto her hips and prepared to battle with Kiril. One single week of peace had passed and now this outside world was erupting into chaos again.

"I will not allow this!"

Kiril looked at her with pity in his dark eyes. "It's not your decision."

Chenoa hissed at him. His words were too soft, just like he was speaking to a child. Well, she was not ignorant!

"They are citizens. You cannot hold them against their will. Enforcer code twenty-eight, section nine."

The junior officer's eyebrows drew down in confusion. Chenoa lifted her chin with pride. Lee's insistence that she rest did have some advantages. Her knowledge of Enforcer law was tripling by the day.

"Very perceptive, Chenoa."

Her husband came up behind her on those silent feet. Chenoa pressed her lips into a tight line. There was no backing down. She couldn't live another day with fear etched onto her heart.

The Commander's face was as hard as she remembered it, his uniform dark and stiff with his authority. Somewhere inside him was the man who brought her body to life. But that side of him he had never shown on his face during the light of day.

Today Chenoa had to reach him.

Three girls stood behind Kiril. They'd crossed right through the open fence. The enforcers had immediately taken them into custody.

"This is unfair. Let my sisters go home." Her husband's eyes glowed like a raptor's in the face of her order. Kiril crossed his arms across his chest denying her demands. Lee shifted his eyes to the women in question as he considered the weight of the decision he had to make.

"You will do nothing of the sort, Commander Tanner." Councilman Welsmon's voice came sailing over the shoulders of the men surrounding Lee.

"We do not want to go home. We want to meet the warriors who guard us."

Her sisters eagerly looked at the men guarding them. Chenoa certainly couldn't fault them for wanting husbands over competitors.

Councilman Welsmon shouldered his way into the confrontation. His eyes glowed with greed as he looked the three women over. He rubbed his palms together as he eyed them from head to toe like prized mares.

"Yes…very nice." The councilman smirked at Kiril. "This will earn you a promotion."

"No, thank you."

"Councilman Welsmon?"

The man swung around with an arrogance that was begging to be smashed. Lee curled his fingers into a fist. "Get the hell off my outpost."

"Now see here, Commander!"

"What I see is a piece of filth that I want off my command before sundown."

"I very much doubt there's a single man under your command stupid enough to carry out that order." The councilman smirked and Lee drew his arm back. Kiril caught his commanding officer's shoulder. Lee turned furious eyes onto the younger man.

"How much time should I give him to pack, sir?"

"Well!" Welsmon sputtered as he shook a finger at both men. Lydia came flying into the fight as fast as her legs would carry her. She aimed a brutal shove at her husband's chest that sent the councilman stumbling backwards.

"Don't you dare get us thrown off this outpost! I swear I won't speak to you ever again!"

"Lydia! No one is tossing me off this compound! I'm going to get these impudent asses thrown out of the ranks!"

Chenoa gasped with horror. She didn't know where the commander ended and her husband began. The councilman's threat was too awful to imagine.

"Robert, you're the ass! I'm staying right here! Do you hear me? And nothing had better change."

Welsmon recovered his composure and grabbed his wife by her forearm. "Relax, darling. You're staying. Commander Tanner can get lost, right after he divorces the Indian. You can have that baby."

Chenoa felt the blood drain from her face. She had never once in her life heard such a hard heart. The councilman raised his cold eyes to hers and smiled. "Besides Lydia, there are three more Indians right there. We can have first pick of them."

"Like hell!" Lee stepped forward and sent the councilman into the sand with a single punch. "You want this uniform? Fine. I'll walk right onto that reservation and live there with my wife if that's the only place I can find people that still respect a marriage."

"I want my own baby." Lydia's voice was almost a whimper. "Do you hear me, Robert? I'll dig in that garden for the next year if that's what it takes."

Chenoa felt the blood rush right back into her face. Lydia looked at the garden with determined resolution as she set her shoulders. She raised her eyes to Chenoa before she turned her back on her husband. "I'm sorry I didn't tell you the truth. Once I heard about Brenda, I was too afraid you would refuse to help me."

The modern woman raised pleading eyes that Chenoa could not ignore. Joy was rushing into her heart in a wave that drowned any anger she might have held for the deception. Lydia did not want to steal her husband! Chenoa felt like she was twirling around like a child in endless circles that made her dizzy with happiness. Chenoa reached for Lydia's hands. "All is well."

"All is not well. Granddaughter!"

Chapter Fourteen

Her grandmother's voice was just as she remembered it. Chenoa turned on her heel and drank in the sight of the leathered faces of her family. Her kin stood amidst her tribe, her lips set into a deep frown. Her eyes ran down Chenoa's body with critical thoroughness. Her sharp eyes settled onto the mound of Chenoa's growing belly as the light of joy entered her dark eyes.

That joy didn't reach the elder Indian woman's face. The younger women who surrounded her tightened their grips on weapons that they aimed at the compound. Chenoa felt her face drain again. Her tribe had come ready to fight. The enforcers reacted to the threat with instant aggression. Weapons appeared on the compound as each man prepared for battle.

"Hold." Lee's voice was as strong as the first time she'd heard it. "Weapons down!"

He cast his eyes over each man under his command. Her grandmother watched him with her sharp eyes. She nodded her head a single time as Lee commanded his men.

"You show me honor where I thought to find none."

Her grandmother nodded again as she took slow steps down to the compound. Her eyes moved over each person 'til they settled onto Nacoma. She raised her hand and motioned the girl forward with a flick of her wrist.

"Let me see your child."

Nacoma hurried to answer the summons. Tadi gurgled happily on her mother's hip. Chenoa's grandmother smiled as she inspected the baby. That smile melted away when she raised her eyes to Nacoma's. "Your family's spirit weeps for you. Go and make amends for causing them grief."

Nacoma dipped her head in respect before she straightened her back and walked up out of the compound.

"It is time for change." Her grandmother's voice was full of her elder authority. "My daughters refuse to give their bodies to the selfish men you present to them. Instead, they seek husbands from those that guard them. It is time we speak upon these matters."

Chenoa felt the weight of her grandmother's eyes return to her. Lee stepped beside her as one of his hands curled around her wrist. It was a solid hold that bound her to his side as he shared the weight of her grandmother's inspection. The public declaration warmed her heart more than any words of love ever could. Lee had disobeyed everything his uniform stood for by letting Nacoma walk back onto her reservation.

But he wouldn't let her leave his side. He stood with his wide shoulders between her armed women of her tribe and her. . His hawk's eyes glowed as he tightened his grip.

"Chenoa is my wife."

"Granddaughter, have you written a promise across your heart?"

"Yes." Yes...yes...yes! It was the most natural thing Chenoa had ever said. Lee moved his hand across her body to rest upon her hip. His strong scent wrapped around her as she settled into his body.

Her grandmother lifted her palm as her voice raised in a soft chant. She held her arms wide and Chenoa flew into them. "My spirit rejoices for you."

Lee watched the embrace and just couldn't help feeling a little left out. Chenoa raised her head as her grandmother turned to leave. Holding his hand out he waited for her to return to his embrace. Her eyes were liquid smooth as she laid her small hand into his. Her grandmother's eyes caught his as he pulled his wife back to his side.

"Now it is well." The old woman retraced her steps to stand with her people. She cast a long look over the compound and the world that had always been hidden from her eyes by the fence. "We will talk again soon?"

"It would be my pleasure." Lee's strong voice made the elder smile before she turned and disappeared over the rise.

The second the last Indian faded from view, Lee swung Chenoa off her feet as he stomped toward their home.

Laughter bubbled up inside her as Lee swung her into their bedroom. His eyes glowed as he once again enjoyed capturing her. They were bound together by a force of nature that drove them toward each other. They would clash again and again as the world around them tried to interfere. The reason was simple. Their spirits were united someplace where words held little meaning.

Lee's mouth lifted in a wolfish grin. "Will you bare your breasts for me?"

"I love you, Husband."

The dress slipped over her shoulders and Lee's eyes stayed settled onto hers instead.

"I don't love you, Chenoa." His hands cupped the sides of her head as he brought his lips within an inch of her face. "I'm obsessed with you. My very life rests inside your grasp and nothing as simple as love can describe that bond."

"Our spirits are united, Husband. It's the purest form of love."

"Maybe it is." Lee took her mouth with his as he dove into the mystery of their union. Somehow he'd discovered that he was incomplete without her. No, love didn't seem to be a large enough word to express that.

But maybe a lifetime together would be.

Epilogue

"Why are they here?"

Her husband wasn't happy about their visitors either. His eyes were mere slits as he glared at the heavy transports unloading on the far side of the compound. Councilman Welsmon was with them and sent Lee a clumsy salute.

Lee nodded his head in acceptance of the respect. There wasn't any warmth to their current relationship but the councilman seemed to be making an attempt at treating Lee with the respect he'd earned.

"That is a medical team. They are the sharpest minds on the globe." Lee turned to look into her eyes as his face showed her his distaste. "They want to study you and any other women on this outpost."

Brenda walked out of her front door and the men unloading supplies froze. Half of them moved toward her as she fell back against her front door with both of her hands over her belly. The councilman yelled at his companions and they turned disappointed looks at him but turned around and left Brenda alone.

Chenoa felt her eyes widen with horror. Her husband caught her chin and turned her eyes back towards his face. "I'll get rid of them if you want me to."

She shook her head and sallowed her distaste. "No, that would be selfish of us."

"Welsmon won't threaten my command again honey, he doesn't have that much authority. You don't have to put up with this."

"Yes, I believe I must." Chenoa smoothed her fingers over her husband's harsh look. "We cannot refuse to help others who want a child. If there is something my body might teach them, I must let them try to learn it."

She placed a kiss on his firm mouth before straightening her back. "Yes, we must, yet I will hope Lydia becomes pregnant soon and save me from their attention."

Enjoy this excerpt from
Dream Specter
© Copyright Mary Wine 2004

Even as tired as she was, Roshelle reacted instantly to the man who ran into the road in front of her car. He just walked from the forest without even glancing to see if there was oncoming traffic. Hitting the brakes only served to slow her vehicle down, she was powerless to stop.

The impact of machine and flesh came with a dull thump. The man rolled up and over her car to land in the road behind her. Roshelle jammed the car into park before pushing her door open and jumping out of the car. Her victim lay on the pavement with a stillness that caused her heart to constrict.

Her fingers found the steady pulse in the column of his neck. She moved her hands over his limbs in search of breaks. His eyes flew open before she finished her assessment.

"Relax…"

He surged upwards from the pavement and brutally flipped her body backwards. Her body slammed into the asphalt with painful force. A knee was jammed across her chest as he leaned enough of his body weight into her chest to cause her to struggle for every breath she drew. One huge hand closed around her neck.

Struggling to draw air into her lungs, Roshelle attempted to force her panic aside. The ease that he threw her over with said he could crush her neck with that single hand. He was drawing rapid breaths as he bent his head down to study her. In the dark his face was nothing more than angles and shadows.

The fingers that encircled her throat suddenly became red hot with pain. It snaked through the five points of contact and straight into her brain. In that single second she felt more exposed than she had ever experienced in her twenty-six years of life. His eyes bore down into her own as she felt the wave wash over her mind before she lost her grip on awareness.

Sitting back on his haunches Jared contemplated the female that was stretched out on the road.

Reaching out he felt along her neck to confirm that he hadn't done irreparable damage to her body. The steady throb of life met with his approval before he hoisted her body onto his shoulder.

"What happened to her?"

"You're late." Jared issued his opinion as more of a judgment to the men that emerged from the darkness. Further comment was interrupted as a truck pulled around the bend in the road. The headlamps lit the scene to near daylight. Jared half-turned and waited for the two occupants of the vehicle to approach him. The men behind him snapped to sharp attention.

The new arrivals returned the briefest of salutes before they dismissed the other men present.

"She alive?" The question was asked with the barest of emotion.

"Yes. This team is inadequate."

An unpleasant look entered both men's eyes as they noted the men in question. There was no room for shortcomings here. Mistakes were often paid for with lives. Tonight they had gotten lucky.

* * * * *

"No! It is not for sale!"

The receiver was dropped back onto the cradle with a loud clunk. Roshelle jumped as the sound set off another wave of pain through her head. She just didn't understand it. Every single fiber of her body ached. She didn't even remember arriving home yesterday. The clock told her that she had slept for fifteen hours, yet she felt more bone weary than she had when she had begun the drive home from the hospital.

But it was the dream that was truly bothering her. She could actually feel the emotions of the dream. It played over and over inside her mind with crystal clearness. Yet she awakened in her own bed so it had to be just the actions of her brain.

Nothing seemed to help lift the fog from her head. It was an effort to even keep her eyes open. Having the Huntley law firm call with yet another insistent offer for her grandmother's property just made her head ache all that much more.

Roshelle would never sell the house that her grandfather built with his own hands. Hacked out of the forest, the four-bedroom home had seen three generations of her family raised up inside its walls.

The increasing level of impatience that Clark Huntley was using was really beginning to rub her raw. Couldn't the man take a hint? Roshelle was home to stay. She had a job and a home. She would think the man would notice that she was making herself quite clear.

"Well, it's never going to be for sale!"

Raising her hand to her forehead, Roshelle rubbed at the pain. Admitting defeat she turned back towards her bedroom. She certainly hoped that she felt better in the morning.

* * * * *

Moving on silent feet, Jared stood beside her bed running his eyes over her body. Her breathing deepened into slow, even breaths as her body relaxed into the deep slumber it needed. Even though she'd only managed to stay on her feet for a few hours, he was impressed.

Probing her mind had been a reflex, born from finding her hands on him in those first few seconds of consciousness. He'd been focused on a trail or he'd been able to recognize her for what she was, a civilian. Jared considered the dark circles that ringed her eyes. His probe had been blunt sending her body into shock from the trauma.

Everything about her looked fragile—from her soft skin, to the gentle curves of her hips. Even her bed looked soft. She'd changed into some flowing bit of nightdress. The material was lying over her body in a delicate wave of ripples. His hand reached for the fabric and let it slip over just the tips of his fingers. So very delicate and feminine.

Sitting on the bed, Jared let their minds mingle. There was an odd ease to it. He was acutely aware of her. It went beyond his psychic abilities. His body joined his mind in the awareness of his new neighbor.

Letting his fingers drift lightly along the curve of her face, he smiled as the skin to skin contact registered. His nerve endings were alight with sensation. She muttered softly turning towards his hand. His palm cupped her cheek as a wave of arousal hit him. It was a steady throb of need that traveled towards his sex.

Abruptly Jared stood up. His blood was pulsing with a tempo that promised him a long night. His staff rose to stiff attention as he let his eyes travel over her soft breasts once more. The nipples were little beads now, lifting the soft fabric of the nightdress to display their tips to him.

The inexperience of his team caused her to become a factor. Making sure his little neighbor recovered was a job he felt compelled to do, but contemplating her body was proving a very annoying distraction.

That was too bad. It wasn't every day that a man got such a delightful new neighbor.

Enjoy this excerpt from
Dream Surrender
© Copyright Mary Wine 2005

Sensation crept up her spine as she noted the sheer size of him. His arms, like his chest, were coated with thick muscle. Even the denim of his jeans betrayed the fact that his legs held the same level of fitness.

It wasn't just his size that captured her attention. There was something not quite tame about him. The way he stood looking out to sea didn't betray that fact—it was an increasing urge she felt to seek shelter. Loren shook her head to dispel her foolishness. If half a glass of champagne was going to her head this much, it was past her bedtime.

Maybe tapping into her emotions was unethical, but at the moment Rourke really didn't care. He was sick of the protocol. Everyone seemed to have an idea on just when and how his psychic sense should be used. What they all missed was the fact that it was a part of him. Sometimes a man's discipline just couldn't hold back his nature.

It was her fault anyway. The way she moved was far too erotic. It wasn't so much the dress she wore, but the way her body moved beneath the fabric. There was a twist and sway to her hips that begged for closer inspection.

Reaching out further, Rourke tapped into her emotions. A smile lifted the corners of his mouth. She was watching him, running her eyes over his body as she considered the desire that was rising up inside her own.

Turning his head, he caught her eyes. Hers widened slightly in surprise, but she brought her emotions under control before he caught the physical signs that her body could give him. But he felt them anyway. Caution was coursing along her nerves as she noticed his interest. The battle she was waging for control, Rourke intended her to lose. Once she discarded the mantle of respectability that her morals were demanding, they could share what promised to be a searing passion.

Loren was never touching another glass of champagne as long as she lived!

She was practically drooling over the man. With her luck tonight, he probably could see it written across her face. Grinding her teeth together, Loren tried to pull herself together enough to walk back to the reception.

The way he stood there watching her made the idea of crossing his path disturbing. Moving her eyes over his form, she marveled at the strength of the man. It floated on the air. It wasn't just his body, it seemed to be deeply rooted inside his being. Her skin was sensitive to the magnetic pull. Her entire body was pulsing with a need that Loren had spent years banishing.

Fascination replaced her misgivings as Loren watched the way he moved. Silently. His body moved across the shoreline with a confidence that confirmed his strength. Loren found herself watching his approach with a intensity that refused to allow her practical instincts any chance to be heard.

With fluid grace, he came closer. Tilting her head back, Loren caught a glimpse of the most startling emerald eyes just seconds before he pulled her body into his with a single movement and his mouth settled onto hers in firm ownership.

Her senses rioted as the sheer volume of impulses overwhelmed them. Too many points of contact sent their signals racing along her nerves into a brain that was struggling to sort them into logical order.

His body moved hers as it pleased, turning and surrounding her flesh as his lips engaged in an assault that demanded complete compliance. The intimate invasion forcing her to yield as his tongue sought her own. Twisting and thrusting, he took her mouth in the way that his body promised to follow. His hips thrust against her, showing her the proof of his intentions.

"Wait… We can't do this!"

"I think we can."

His voice held as much iron as his body did, the deep, determined tone settling over her ears. Her own inability to deny the truth of her mutual interest caused true fear to rise up inside her.

Loren sighed as her fingertips became ultrasensitive. Her hands traveled across the shirt-covered expanse of his chest. She ran her hands back and forth over his chest as her fingertips delighted with the hard muscle they found. Longing sprang up as she tried to force her brain to function.

"I can't do this."

Pulling his head up, Rourke considered the female in his arms. He could smell the passion on her body, feel it seeping into the pores of his skin. At the moment the sand beneath them would serve just fine. The panic in her voice was the only thing causing him to question his purpose.

Searching her thoughts, he considered what he found. If she had a boyfriend at that reception, her feelings didn't run very deep. No, her concern stemmed from the strength of her own arousal.

Lowering his mouth again, Rourke took possession of her lips. He captured the moan that escaped from her as she lost her battle to ignore their mutual attraction. Her body leapt as passion ignited inside it. Her hips twisted into his as her hands moved over him in blatant invitation.

Thoughts simply refused to form. Loren couldn't stop her hands and she didn't try. He just smelled so very male. It was intoxicating in its intensity. His body was so hard. She was craving it. Her fingers clawed at his shirt searching for the skin she could smell.

"Come with me."

He pulled her by their joined hands a full thirty feet before her mind cleared enough to offer protest. Digging her feet into the sand, she pulled him to a halt.

"Right here is fine with me."

"No!" This time the sounds from the wedding reception intruded on her reckless behavior with stinging awareness.

Loren thrust her passion aside, grabbing at the control she'd somehow lost.

"I can not do this." Forcing each word out, Loren used their truth to steady her resolve.

"Whoever he is, I'd say it's time to break it off."

"It's not that simple."

"The truth is always simple. It's when you start to deceive yourself that things get complicated."

Their hands were still joined. Loren stared at his flesh as it imprisoned hers and lamented the facts that would limit her to this last taste of him. What her body demanded just could never be.

"I agree, but some things are just not meant to happen."

The longing in her eyes caused Rourke to hesitate before replying. Maybe she was afraid of breaking up with the guy.

"I won't let him hurt you."

One quick step and a simple twist broke the hold on her hand. Moving further away she turned to survey her companion. Forcing her eyes to take in the aggression in his, she coupled it with the harsh lesson that life had taught her long ago. Men always manipulated women to suit their needs. This one was no different. He'd protect her 'till he became bored, then she'd be on her own.

"I can take care of myself."

"No, honey, what you need only I can take care of."

About the author:

I write to reassure myself that reality really is survivable. Between traffic jams and children's sporting schedules, there is romance lurking for anyone with the imagination to find it.

I spend my days making corsets and petticoats as a historical costumer. If you send me an invitation marked formal dress, you'd better give a date or I just might show up wearing my bustle.

I love to read a good romance and with the completion of my first novel, I've discovered I am addicted to writing these stories as well.

Dream big or you might never get beyond your front yard.

Mary welcomes mail from readers. You can write to her c/o Ellora's Cave Publishing at 1337 Commerce Drive, Suite 13, Stow OH 44224.

Why an electronic book?

We live in the Information Age—an exciting time in the history of human civilization in which technology rules supreme and continues to progress in leaps and bounds every minute of every hour of every day. For a multitude of reasons, more and more avid literary fans are opting to purchase e-books instead of paperbacks. The question to those not yet initiated to the world of electronic reading is simply: *why?*

1. *Price.* An electronic title at Ellora's Cave Publishing and Cerridwen Press runs anywhere from 40-75% less than the cover price of the <u>exact same title</u> in paperback format. Why? Cold mathematics. It is less expensive to publish an e-book than it is to publish a paperback, so the savings are passed along to the consumer.

2. *Space.* Running out of room to house your paperback books? That is one worry you will never have with electronic novels. For a low one-time cost, you can purchase a handheld computer designed specifically for e-reading purposes. Many e-readers are larger than the average handheld, giving you plenty of screen room. Better yet, hundreds of titles can be stored within your new library—a single microchip. (Please note that Ellora's Cave and Cerridwen Press does not endorse any specific brands. You can check our website at www.ellorascave.com or

www.cerridwenpress.com for customer recommendations we make available to new consumers.)

3. *Mobility.* Because your new library now consists of only a microchip, your entire cache of books can be taken with you wherever you go.

4. *Personal preferences are accounted for.* Are the words you are currently reading too small? Too large? Too...**ANNOYING**? Paperback books cannot be modified according to personal preferences, but e-books can.

5. *Instant gratification.* Is it the middle of the night and all the bookstores are closed? Are you tired of waiting days—sometimes weeks—for online and offline bookstores to ship the novels you bought? Ellora's Cave Publishing sells instantaneous downloads 24 hours a day, 7 days a week, 365 days a year. Our e-book delivery system is 100% automated, meaning your order is filled as soon as you pay for it.

Those are a few of the top reasons why electronic novels are displacing paperbacks for many an avid reader. As always, Ellora's Cave and Cerridwen Press welcomes your questions and comments. We invite you to email us at service@ellorascave.com, service@cerridwenpress.com or write to us directly at: 1056 Home Ave. Akron OH 44310-3502.